The
White
Peacock

The White Peacock

by
Mary Linn Roby

HAWTHORN BOOKS, INC.
PUBLISHERS/*New York*

THE WHITE PEACOCK

Dedicated to
Katharine Kidde

The
White
Peacock

CHAPTER

I

"You realize, I hope, that my aunt won't be an easy person to deal with," Marian Russell said, maneuvering the red Austin skillfully through a village square lined with canvas-covered stalls and crowded with peasants. "She's been an expatriate for years. Portugal is her home now in every sense, but she still manages to remain a fine example of vintage British eccentricity. I'm only trying to say that you shouldn't take her too seriously."

I murmured something, uncomfortably aware that I was too tired to listen properly to what this woman was saying. My plane had landed in Lisbon that morning, and I had tried to see too much in the few hours before I was to leave for the northern part of the country. I had eaten green Portuguese oysters at the Floresta and walked about the harbor, watching gaily dressed women carrying baskets of silverfish on their heads as they climbed barefoot up the precipitous streets that led from the harbor. I had

seen the magnificent bronze equestrian statue of King
John I in the Black Horse Square and heard the screaming
of the peacocks on the grounds of the Castilo, which
looms over the capital city. And in the afternoon at five
I had wandered into an arena on the outskirts of the city
and seen a young matador nearly impaled on the horns
of an angry bull. There had been too many new sights
and sounds for a single day, and now I was reacting as
any tourist might react. The only problem was that I was
not a tourist.

"It slows us down, having to drive through these villages," the woman beside me said. "Unfortunately there's
no other route to Alcombra. That's one of the things my
aunt likes best about the estate. It's so isolated that not
even her family can come to see her often."

The bitterness in her voice roused me. Half turning on
the seat, I saw her profile: sharp-nosed, imperious, her
deep-set eyes half visible from the side under thick dark
glasses. She had, I suspected, once been beautiful, but
now the skin of her face hung in tiny loose folds, like
crumpled paper. She was about fifty, I guessed, although
she looked older in the harsh blazing light of the afternoon. She had done everything that a woman can do to
make herself younger. Her hair was skillfully tinted,
clinging like a soft cap to her small head. Her beautifully
cut silk dress clung to a figure as slim as a girl's. But one
could not escape the grotesquery of that crushed face. I
had never met her before she had picked me up at the
Hotel Aviz as had been prearranged. That had been only
half an hour before, and already I was aware that she
was a deeply unhappy woman.

We were driving out of the market town now. The road
was a steep alley that wove its way between narrow stone
houses jammed into the hillside about which the town was
built. From the upper windows brightly colored laundry
hung like flags on lines that stretched across the cobbled
street. Old women in black pressed back against the walls

as we passed, eyeing us curiously. A peasant leading a mule up the narrow road before us gave up the right of way reluctantly, and through the open windows I could hear him shouting something after us. Still the road wound up until suddenly I saw a castle looming against the sky. There seemed to be castles everywhere in this country, pushing their walls out of the boulders as though they were an extension of the stone itself.

"Do you live with your aunt at Alcombra?" I asked her, aware that I should say something. If it were night, it would have been easier to close my eyes and doze surreptitiously. As it was, I had to keep myself alert any way that I could, even if it meant asking questions about relationships that, in a sense, did not concern me. The London solicitor who had made the arrangements for me to come to Alcombra had made it quite clear that it was the wish of the owner that the inventory be completed as quickly as possible, and that to facilitate this, I would be left quite alone to get about it.

The woman beside me laughed harshly. "The only people my aunt trusts are the people she hires. When you pay someone, you can tell them what to do—when to smile, what to say—and when you don't want them around anymore, you can tell them to go away, and they'll go. Servants aren't really people, according to my aunt. They're extensions of her ego, and she likes that. Oh, she really likes that."

She broke off and turned to stare at me through the two sheets of dark glass that covered her eyes. "Did you notice," she said, "how I managed to avoid answering your question directly? That's one of the many little things my aunt loathes about me. I'm inclined to hedge. The fact is that I don't live with her. She wouldn't have me, even if I'd agree to come. I'm only at Alcombra now because she's dying."

I stared at her incredulously. "But I was told——"

"You were told whatever she wanted you to be told,

and no more. You can count on that. Give me a cigarette, will you? You'll find a pack in my handbag."

The bag, like everything else about this woman, was expensive and in good taste. Distracted for the moment, I fumbled inside it for the cigarette, pushing aside a gold compact, a vial of perfume, a soft linen handkerchief with thickly embroidered edges, and a wallet fat with bills.

"Light it for me, will you?" the woman said sharply as I pulled out the pack. "I'm not that familiar with this wretched road."

We were high above the village now. The brown-tiled rooftops sprawled under the golden fingers of the sinking sun. Huge boulders jutted from the almost sheer drop at the side of the road. To our right rose the battlements of the castle. The woman beside me took the cigarette and leaned over the wheel, her eyes intent on the twisting, narrow road. And then, suddenly, we reached the peak, and in the distance in front of us there stretched a broad plain spotted with groves of olive trees and cork oaks. Beyond them a broad river cut a blue gash in the earth.

"That's the Mondego," Marian Russell said in a low voice. "Beyond it is another river, the Douro. You can see the Douro from Alcombra. This part of Portugal is one of the most beautiful places in the world. Sometimes I think that if I didn't hate her so much, I'd never want to leave it. But I'm a bit old for that sort of romantic nonsense, aren't I? A bit old for a good many things, according to her."

I would have made the monologue into a dialogue if I had known how. Obviously this woman hated her aunt. Obviously, too, she did not care who knew it—or, perhaps, for reasons of her own, she wanted to make it perfectly clear to me from the start what her position in the household was.

"Her solicitor told me that she was ill," I said, "but I didn't realize that she was dying."

"That's the reason that she feels she has to have the collection inventoried at once," Marian Russell said in a tight voice. A battered station wagon hove into sight as we rounded a corkscrew turn, and I heard her swear under her breath as she wrenched the car as close as she could to the boulders that lined our side of the narrow road. The station wagon lurched past us in a cloud of dust, and for a moment I thought that it would surely plunge into the gulf below. I caught my breath.

"She could have sent the chauffeur to pick you up," the woman beside me muttered, bending over the wheel and edging the car around another hairpin turn. "She knows how I hate driving on these roads. It's her idea of a subtle kind of punishment."

"Punishment for what?" There was something about the constant complaint in her voice that was beginning to annoy me.

"For coming to Alcombra. We all came, you see—as soon as we heard. All of what's left of the so-called family. Like vultures. That's what she calls us: vultures waiting to pick her bones."

Now the road plunged down toward the plain below in a long silver line, and I felt myself relax.

"You're a good deal younger than I thought you would be," Marian Russell said, changing the subject with a disconcerting rapidity as she pressed her foot harder on the accelerator. "Is it true that you have your own gallery in London?"

"Yes," I said, relieved that we had abandoned the topic of vultures. "It was my father's. He died two years ago."

"And you're a specialist on Iberian art?"

"It's what I deal in primarily, yes."

My companion flicked her cigarette out the window. "What made you agree to come here and do the inventory?" she demanded. "Did she offer you a sizable commission? You don't have to answer that if you don't want. It's probably unpardonably rude of me to ask, but you'll find that our family is always interested in the subject of money—particularly money that we won't be inheriting."

It was becoming hotter and hotter as we plunged down toward the plain. Even the mimosa beside the road seemed to shrivel in the heat. Now that we had nearly reached the bottom of the mountain, the road veered to the west, and the red glow of the sinking sun seemed to burn my face. I pulled my long hair off my neck, coiled it into a bun, and dug in my handbag for a clasp—deliberately delaying. Certainly I did not want to tell this woman the real reason why I had come here. It remained to sort over in my mind other possible reasons that she might accept. As for the question concerning the commission, she was right. I had no intention of answering that. From what she had said it was clear that she and the other relatives would begrudge even a normal commission, which was all I was receiving.

"Lady Stewart's collection is well known," I said slowly. "Anyone who's interested in Iberian art would be interested in examining it. As far as I know, no one has been allowed to see it for the past thirty years, at least. There are rumors, but that's all. That sort of situation was bound to intrigue anyone in my field."

We had reached the flatness of the plain now. In a grove of cork oaks men worked at stripping the bark from the thick branches. Around the base of the trees, oats bent red-gold heads to the sun. Oxen pulling carts full of drying cork lumbered along the side of the road. There was something soothing about the peacefulness of the scene. It was a sharp contrast to Lisbon, and an even sharper contrast, I guessed, to what would await me at Alcombra.

"I hope," Marian Russell said in a voice sharp with amusement, "that you didn't delude yourself into thinking that my aunt would let you have first pick of a few things. I mean, you aren't laboring under the misconception that she's going to do the sensible thing and sell the lot?"

"I understood that she intended to turn Alcombra into a museum," I said, stung by the implication of what this woman was suggesting. "I was told that nothing was to be sold."

"That's the way the situation stands now!" Marian Russell snapped. "Obviously it's an insane idea. The will can't be allowed to stand."

We turned to look at one another at the same moment. Above and below the dark glasses her face sagged in unattractive lines. I wondered how long it had been since she had laughed. Perhaps it was unfair to blame her. Perhaps she had had good reason to let bitterness consume her. For that matter, so had I.

"You'd rather I wasn't as frank, wouldn't you?" she asked, turning back to the road. "I suspect that you aren't particularly enthusiastic about self-revelation, Miss Haverlock—either your own or anyone else's—but you're going to have to take sides as soon as you reach Alcombra. You might as well know that in advance."

There was an arbitrary way about the way she treated me that infuriated me. I did not want to be analyzed, particularly not by someone who had known me a little over an hour. It had been difficult enough for me to have let Philip dissect me emotionally, to examine all my responses with microscopic care. In the end I had not been able to cope with that. Never again would I allow anyone to understand me as well as he had, because I knew now that there was no greater humiliation than in being understood.

"I don't know exactly what you mean by taking sides, Miss Russell," I said sharply. "It doesn't matter to me what you tell or don't tell me. I'm here to do an inventory, and that's all."

"In other words, you're my aunt's hireling," she taunted me.

"Yes," I said. "That's as good a word as any other. Why, what do you want me to be? Some sort of moral arbiter?"

She had not expected the attack, and I saw her hands tighten on the wheel. "Now you're angry," she said in a low voice. "I seem to have a certain flair for antagonizing people."

We had reached the banks of the river now. From the distance, perhaps because it reflected the sky, the river seemed blue, but now it lay before us like a strip of brown satin, skirted with yellow sandbanks. We crossed an arched stone bridge that spanned the sluggish, reed-spotted waters at a narrow point and found ourselves speeding past an orange grove, the ripe fruit hanging like small suns among the lush green leaves.

"I suppose I should apologize," the woman beside me said in a low voice. "I can't expect you to spend your life waiting for something, and then at the last minute to see all your hopes disappear in thin air. All that's left is the hatred, you see, and I can't bear what that's doing to me. What it's doing to all of us."

We were crossing the Seira da Gralheira range when the brakes of the Austin gave way. We had driven in silence since we had passed the Mondego, crossing fertile plains filled with prosperous looking vineyards, through an ancient town surrounded by chestnut trees, crossing the Douro over a curiously arched medieval bridge. The woman beside me seemed to see nothing but the road in front of her. Her mouth was grim. Obviously she was angry, although whether with me or with herself I was not certain. There had been times in my life when I, too, had rushed into intimacy too soon, as she had done. It was obvious that she was in no emotional condition to make valid decisions. Her nerves were brittle. I did not have to know the details to understand why. She had obviously waited for a long time, with the promise of her aunt's wealth glowing in the future. It was the sort of prospect which might have softened the blow of personal disappointments, such as her fading beauty. And now there were no more prospects at a time in her life when she needed them most. I knew enough about her aunt's affairs to be certain that there would be little set aside for the heirs to divide, despite the rumored value of her collection.

The solicitor who had contacted me in London was efficient but scarcely a master of conciseness. "Lady Stewart always makes her wishes very well known," he had told me, tapping his pencil against his goateed chin as he leaned across his desk, his spectacled blue eyes taking in every detail about me with obvious relish. "She has not lived in England for thirty years," he continued, his thin voice beating a staccato of sound against the silence of the dusty office. "However, our firm has continued to serve her through the years, and I do not think I am boasting when I say that we understand her particular—er—viewpoints, some of which are not absolutely conventional, let us say."

He had gone on then to tell me about her plans to establish a museum at Alcombra. "She knows, of course, that she has a limited time to take care of these details," he had said, and then he had colored and gone on to the subject of what would be demanded from me. I understood now the slip he had made. He had nearly told me that the old woman was about to die, but for some reason he must have been directed not to disclose that fact.

"Lady Stewart has spent her entire adult life collecting paintings and objets d'art, as I'm sure you know," the solicitor had told me. "At our insistence she has always kept a certain reserve of capital on hand, but every other shilling has gone into the upkeep of the estate in Portugal and the purchase of items of value. Actually, very little money has gone into Alcombra, in the sense that the estate takes care of itself. It possesses one of the largest vineyards in the Douro country, you see. Alcombra port is well known." He pressed his lips together as though savoring a remembered taste. "Lady Stewart is kind enough to send along several bottles every year at Christmas time. Not that she takes much interest in the vineyards and the bottling and all the rest of it. That was her husband's contribution. Now he's dead, of course, but there's an excellent manager, I understand, and the business carries on. Ah, yes, it carries on."

The light in his eyes had faded, and he sat isolated with his own thoughts until I tapped his hand to remind him of my presence. It had all been rather amusing, or perhaps I was simply trying hard to make everything in my life seem amusing. The idea of getting away from London for a few weeks had been especially tempting. Philip and I had the same friends. It was an effort to keep from meeting him accidentally. I had recently taken on an experienced assistant who was perfectly capable of keeping the gallery on Bond Street open. The commission that Lady Stewart offered was not particularly substantial, but there had been the temptation to examine the hoard that this legendary woman had spent a lifetime collecting. I had not lied when I had told Marian Russell that that had been my motive for coming. It was simply that there were other reasons as well—deeply personal reasons—and I would have to explain all of that to her if I were to make her understand why I did not want to become involved in the internecine struggles that were apparently going on at Alcombra.

So I had remained silent as we had driven through the fading sunlight, the road rising steadily through pine-shadowed hills. We had stopped once, just as the sun was setting, at an inn, a long, low stone building with pastel-shaded walls of pink and cream, the windows bordered with boxes of scarlet geraniums. Men in rusty black sat sipping wine at outdoor tables, and childen with great bunches of poppies in their arms had surrounded us as we had ordered, offering the scarlet flowers for sale. It had been as peaceful as a scene painted by Patinir, but the tension between me and the chic, worn-faced woman who was my companion had been too great to break with casual words. I knew that she thought me cold, disinterested. I pitied her, but I did not want to become involved in anyone else's life—not now. I had come here for one purpose—the inventory—and I was determined that that was all there was to be to it.

I was dozing when I suddenly became aware that something was wrong. It was night, and the headlights of the little car thrust thin saffron fingers into the darkness, illuminating a narrow mountain road that seemed to plunge precipitously into a black void into which we were moving with frightening speed.

"It's the brakes," Marian said in a shrill voice. "They won't take!"

In the light of the dashboard I saw her wrench the wheel to the right as we approached a curve. I was thrown violently against the door. The moment seemed to suspend itself in time.

"Pump the brake pedal!" I cried.

She must have done what I told her to do, because the car began to slow. At the same moment the road seemed to level. There was a slight rise ahead. Beyond it lay nothing, and I knew that this was only a pause in the descent. We had to stop the car now, before the top of the rise.

"Pull on the emergency brake!" I said.

The woman beside me did not respond. I saw her bend over the wheel, staring into the beams of light. She saw, as I had, that in a moment we would be headed downward again, and yet she seemed to be incapable of responding. Reaching out, I pulled back the stick of the emergency brake with all my strength. The car came to a screeching halt, throwing both of us violently forward. I felt my head strike the dashboard, and then for a moment I was aware of nothing but the heavy warmth of the night air, and the silence.

Pulling myself back onto my seat, I turned and saw the woman beside me slumped over the wheel.

"Are you all right?" I asked.

She made no response. At first I had the absurd thought that she was stubbornly determined to maintain her angry silence, but it was not simply that she did not speak. She did not move either, and I was aware of a tiny thorn-prick of fear. Until that moment everything had happened too fast for me to be aware of fear—if fear was there—but now, when the real danger seemed to be past, I was afraid.

I took her gently by the shoulders and pulled her back from the wheel. There was not enough light, and it was only when her head was against the back of the seat that I could see that she was unconscious, her eyes closed, a trickle of blood running like a black line across her right cheek.

I have never been particularly good in emergencies. My mind seems to stop functioning. My only instinct is to find someone to help. And that was what I did then, even though reason would have told me that I was not likely to find anyone on the side of what appeared to be an uninhabited mountain at that time of night.

The futility of what I was doing struck me as soon as I stood beside the car, staring past the headlights at what I knew must be the edge of the sheer cliff that rimmed the road. And yet what else could I do? Even to move her would be risky. I had no way of knowing if she had suffered internal injuries, and yet I would have to pull her onto the other seat if I wanted to risk driving the car down what was left of the torturous road. Perhaps with the emergency brake half on, I could make it, even though it would burn out the brake linings. Still, I did not know this place. I was as likely to drive the car off the edge of the road as to reach the bottom of the mountain safely.

And once at the bottom, how could I be sure that there would be houses, a village? I did not even know how far we were from Alcombra.

The only other alternative besides remaining there, doing what I could for her and waiting for a car, which might not come for hours, was obviously to go on down the road on foot and try to find a house, a phone. Or perhaps it would be better to go back. Because I had been asleep until the moment when the brakes had begun to fail, I had no idea what we had passed as we had come up the mountain. For all I knew there might be a village somewhere behind me, its lights hidden by the boulders whose bulk merged with the night sky.

Certain that anything I might do would be wrong, I turned and saw a tiny pinpoint of light flare in the darkness above me. In the same moment there came the sound of rocks falling. One of them struck the car. I cried out, startled. Silence answered me. And then I became aware that something or someone was sliding down the rock surface toward the back of the car. I clasped my hands to my mouth and saw the shape of a man emerge on the road. Slowly he came toward me. It was not until he was beside me that I could see his face, fractured by the glow of the headlights. He was young, and there was nothing in his face of the square Celtic quality of the Portuguese. His blond hair was cut low on his forehead, the eyes deep set. He was wearing slacks and a light pullover sweater, and a knapsack was strapped to his broad shoulders.

"My God," he said in English, with a strong British accent, "I didn't know that anyone was here. Look, I can see that I've frightened you. I'm sorry. I was lighting a candle at a shrine up there—no special reason, but it amuses me. I often stop and do that when I'm traveling at night."

I drew my hands away from my mouth and nodded, aware of a great surge of relief. I knew the sort of shrine he meant. Tiny octagonal chapels sheltering stone figures showing scenes from the Passion dotted the mountainsides. When we had crossed the Douro, I had seen a woman in black kneeling at one of them. It was, I thought, a strange thing for a young hitchhiker to do at night—or in the day, for that matter—but there was something about the openness of this man's face which reassured me.

The stranger smiled. "I assume," he said, "you didn't stop up here for the view. What's wrong? Car trouble?"

"The brakes gave way," I said and found that my voice was hoarse, as though I had not used it in a long time. I moistened my lips. "We nearly went off the road."

"We? Do you mean that your husband's gone for help?"

"No. The woman I'm with. . . . She's inside the car. I pulled on the emergency brake to stop us, and she must have struck her head against the wheel. She's unconscious. I didn't know what. . . ."

He was no longer listening to me. Unloosening his knapsack, he threw it on the ground and slid into the front seat of the car.

"She's still out," I heard him say. "Not much bleeding. It feels as though there's a cut on her forehead. Listen. Reach inside my sack. There's a flashlight in there. And a flask of water."

I did what he told me, awkwardly, discovering that my hands were trembling. There was a book in the knapsack and a shirt. A package of sandwiches. I found the flashlight at the bottom and the flask. By the time I handed them to him, my hands were steady.

"All right," he said. "Now, take this handkerchief and pour some water on it."

He kept on talking as I uncapped the flask and tilted it over the square of white linen. Through the open door I could see him bending over Marian, shining the flashlight on her. "She'll be all right, I think," I heard him say. "She couldn't have struck her head very hard, or she would have had more of a concussion. Here, give me that handkerchief. That's right. I'll just put it on her forehead, folded so. That's right. I don't suppose you have any wine. Brandy. Odd sort of thing to be without when you need it in this part of the country, but I don't suppose two women traveling alone. . . . Is she your mother?"

The question startled me. Despite her lined face, I did not associate the intense woman slumped against the seat with motherhood.

"No," I muttered. "She's—she's a friend. An acquaintance really. But I can't bear to think of anything serious happening to her. I mean, it was my fault. I pulled the emergency."

"You didn't have much choice, did you?" the stranger said. "Not if the brakes are gone. It's better to have her concussed than both of you dead."

The narrowness of our escape had not struck me with full force until that moment. My legs suddenly threatened not to support me, and I leaned against the car.

"Look here," the young man said. "I don't like this. She should be coming to by now. How long had she been unconscious before I came along?"

"Not more than a few minutes," I murmured.

"Then this must have been the car that passed me up there," he mused. "Driving like a bat, she was. Don't think she saw me. I had to jump out of the way. It was your headlights that picked out the shrine for me. Does she always drive like that?"

"I don't know," I said. "We only met today. Perhaps the brakes had just begun to give way. I was asleep. But that doesn't matter now. What if she's seriously hurt? We've got to get her to a doctor."

"You don't know this part of the country, do you?" the young man said, turning to me. "The nearest town large enough to have a doctor must be twenty-five miles away, and the roads are like this most of the way."

"It's better than staying here," I said. And then, remembering: "But we can't drive the car anyway, not with the brakes gone."

"We'll be all right if we put it in first gear," he said. "Do you want me to drive? We'll get her in the back seat. You can sit in there with her and keep putting water on her forehead. That's all we can do."

He was right. It was all we could do. I watched him move the woman into the back seat as gently as though she were a child.

"That's right," he said. "You sit in that corner. Here, put her head on your lap."

Marian groaned.

"You see," he said. "She's going to be all right. You don't have to look like that."

Leaning across the seat, he put his hand on my arm. "It's going to be all right," he said. "You'll see. Look, before we start off, I'd better introduce myself. I'm David Ashor."

I tried to smile. "I'm Irene Haverlock."

"It's a great pleasure, senhora." He tugged at his forelock as I had seen peasants do. I felt a warm glow of gratitude. He was trying hard to make me relax, and, to a degree, he was succeeding.

"Now, one other thing," he said briskly. "The closest town is behind us, and that means negotiating the rest of this road and then turning around and coming back up it again. Where were you two going, anyway?"

"It's a country estate," I said. "Not too far from here, I think. It's called Alcombra."

For a moment he did not speak. In the light of the dashboard I saw his face suddenly grow set. The smile faded.

"Life is full of little surprises, isn't it?" he said, turning away from me, his voice grim. "Perhaps I should have guessed. As it happens, I'm on my way to Alcombra, too."

It was not until David Ashor had worked the car laboriously down the mountainside in first gear that he spoke again, and then the note of reassurance had returned to his voice.

"It's only about ten miles now to Alcombra," he said, "and on a straightaway we can make better time. Has she shown any signs of coming to?"

I pressed the damp cloth closer to the forehead of the woman whose head was cradled in my lap. "No," I said, "but she's breathing evenly, as though she were asleep."

The car picked up speed. In the glare of the headlights I could just see the even pattern of a narrow road, bordered with pine trees. The air coming through the open windows was cool, and I sensed that the descent from the mountain had not been as great as the original climb. We were, I thought, on some sort of plateau, apparently uninhabited. It was not so late that there would not be lights shining from houses if we were passing them. I felt a great sense of isolation, mixed with the ache of an anxiety that was not completely caused by what had happened to Marian Russell. There was exhaustion, too. I was tense enough so that it did not encompass me, but I felt it lurking inside. I did not want to think. I sensed that if I tried to examine the implications of what had happened, I might panic. And it was not the time for panic.

"Have you been to Alcombra before?" I asked the man in front of me. I did not want to be the one to ask questions, but I could not bear the silence.

"Many times," he said. "I should have explained. You see, I'm Lady Stewart's nephew—grandnephew, actually. She doesn't have what you'd call a strong family sense, but when I was a boy, I spent my vacations here. Partly because there was no other place to go. Partly because, I think, she wanted me."

I stared at the back of his head, bewildered. If both he and Marian Russell were who they claimed to be, how had it been that he had not appeared to recognize her? She had said that the family was descending on Alcombra like vultures. Was that his role, too? It did not seem to fit with what I had seen of his character, but then, people were seldom what they seemed to be. By this time I should have known that lesson by heart.

"What about you?" I heard him say. "Are you part of the family, too?"

"Wouldn't you know if I were?"

"Believe it or not, besides her stepson, William, I've met only one stray uncle who tried to force a visit on Aunt Lelia when I was staying there once. She sent him packing." He laughed. "The others either didn't try to come or were there when I wasn't. I don't know. Aunt Lelia always claimed it made her ill to think about her relatives, let alone discuss them."

It was an explanation of my unasked question—a rational answer, based on what I already knew of his great-aunt, Lady Stewart. And still I found myself wondering if the answer had not come a little too smoothly.

"If you're not a relative then, do you mind my asking who you are?"

"I suppose you could call me an art dealer," I said. "I have a small gallery in London."

He whistled through his teeth. "You mean my aunt is going to part with some of her collection? I don't believe it."

"No," I said. "I've come here to make an inventory. That's all."

"That surprises me, too," he said. "She's always talked about having that done, but she's always put it off, because, quite frankly, I don't think she likes to have strangers in the house. Particularly people who might realize the value of what she has there. I mean, she's talked a lot to me about making Alcombra a museum, but only after she's dead. As long as she's alive, she seems to want to keep it to herself. It's one of her little peculiarities."

When Marian Russell had spoken of her aunt's eccentricity, there had been an underlying viciousness in her voice, as though she would have rather referred to it as a manifestation of an unbalanced mind. With David it was obviously different. His tone was one of indulgence. It came to me, suddenly, that he might not know that Lady Stewart was ill.

"I think," I said carefully, "that your great-aunt is convinced now that the inventory ought to be done immediately."

"Why?" The road began to wind again, and I saw him grip the wheel tightly. His voice told me that he was only half concentrating on what we were saying.

"We aren't going up another mountain, are we?" I asked, catching my breath.

"In a way—but only halfway up. The house overlooks a valley. Don't worry. As long as we aren't going downhill, there's no danger. Can you tell me why the inventory has to be done now?"

"How long has it been since you've seen your great-aunt?" I hedged.

"Nearly a year now. I'm at Oxford, you see, doing graduate work. I have a fellowship. It's been quite a few months since I've been able to afford to take any time off. Then, instead of coming straight here, I took a walking tour of Spain. It's something I've always wanted to do."

"But she knows you're coming?"

"We don't correspond. Letters are almost as much of an intrusion as people as far as Aunt Lelia is concerned. Why? Has anything happened?"

"She's been ill apparently," I said.

"You mean she's dying?" He shot the words at me over his shoulder. It was almost as though he were challenging me.

"I—I don't know," I said. "I was told. . . ."

I broke off as the unconscious woman began to groan

again. I felt her eyelashes flicker under my fingers, and she began to roll her head back and forth in my lap.

"She's coming to," I murmured. "There, it's all right. Everything's all right."

"What happened?" I could scarcely hear her voice. I bent over her. Her face was a white oval in the darkness.

"You struck your head on the wheel when the car stopped," I said. "You've been unconscious."

Her hands pushed mine aside. "My head aches," she groaned. "I'm so sleepy."

She was not, I realized, alert enough to realize that the car was moving. She was dazed, able to think only about how she was feeling.

"Get her to sit up," I heard David say in a low voice. "If she's had a concussion, we shouldn't let her go to sleep."

If she heard his voice, she gave no sign. "Listen to me," I murmured, my lips close to her face. "Can you sit up?"

She did not answer me. I could not see whether her eyes were open or not. I brushed a finger over them and found them closed. Her breathing was heavy and slow.

"She's unconscious again," I said, "or sleeping."

"Push her into an upright position," David said crisply. "Try to get her to open her eyes. Put more water on her face. You have the flask, haven't you? Slap her if you have to, but keep her awake."

She was heavier than she looked, but I managed to make her sit up. The water did no good. I struck her once, gently, and then harder, stinging my fingers on her cheek. Her head lolled back against the cushions. There was no response.

"It's no good," I told him.

I heard him take a deep breath. "All right," he said. "I'm going to turn the car off the road and walk her. She's not complaining of pain anywhere but in her head. I don't think, considering what happened, that she could have any internal injuries. I may be wrong. You can argue with me if you want to, but I think she ought to be kept awake."

"I don't know," I said. "I just don't know. You said the house was only about ten miles farther on. Perhaps we ought to just keep going."

"Perhaps you're right. We aren't making very good time, but we ought to be there in another twenty minutes. Aunt Lelia's companion will know what to do. She's a gargoyle type, but she's a pretty competent nurse when she has to be. Her first reaction will probably be that we shouldn't have brought a stranger to Alcombra no matter what the reason, but I can talk her out of that."

"Miss Russell isn't a stranger," I said. "She's staying at the house."

"Russell!" He turned to face me, and for a moment he lost control of the car, which veered toward the side of the road. I cried out, and he jerked the wheel just in time to prevent us from striking a stone wall that formed a sort of terrace to our right.

"Russell?" he said again.

"Marian Russell," I said. "She must be one of those relatives you don't know. She told me she was Lady Stewart's niece. That makes her your aunt, doesn't it?"

"Does it?" His voice was tight with anger. We were going faster now, taking the curves wide. It was obvious that finding out who the unconscious woman was had upset him, but I had no idea why. I tried to tell myself it did not matter. I had been able to disassociate myself from Marian's problems. I had told myself I did not care about her bitterness and the reason for it, but somehow with David it was different. Perhaps it was because the woman had tried to confide in me. Obviously he had no intention of doing that, and yet I felt myself wishing that he would. I wanted to understand what had upset him.

"What's happening?" Marian Russell's voice was thick.

Now that she was sitting up, I could see her face more clearly. Her eyes were open.

"Talk to her." David's voice was grim. "Keep her awake."

"Who's that?" she said weakly. "Who's driving the car? Where are we going? Oh, my God, how my head aches."

"We'll be at Alcombra in a few minutes," I told her. "Everything is all right."

"Who's driving?" she repeated. Her voice was stronger now. I took her hand and began to rub it, but she pulled away from me.

"I came along just after the accident," David said before I could answer. "I'm taking you home."

"Who—who are you?"

I saw David shake his head slowly from side to side, and I knew that he was warning me not to answer her.

"I'm a hitchhiker," he said. "Just someone looking for a job harvesting grapes."

"But you're—you're British."

"The British hitchhike, too," he muttered. "Don't bother too much about me. All I'm concerned with is getting you home safely."

Suddenly she was reaching for my hand. Her fingers were like ice.

"Is he telling the truth?" she whispered. "Is he really taking us to Alcombra?"

"Yes," I said. "You don't have to worry."

There was a long pause. "But he doesn't know the way," she protested. Her voice was thick again, and her head swayed back against the seat. "It's not easy to find if you don't know the way."

"Tell her I'll find it," David snapped. "Tell her not to worry."

Without warning, he switched on the car radio. The strains of guitar music split the silence. They were playing a fado, and in a moment a woman picked up the lament, her voice rising and falling through the quivering static. The thick swish of her Portuguese filled the car:

> Don't speak to me of that street,
> The street
> That for me was the loveliest of all
> And still is.
>
> Yes, I'd rather you kept silent.
> Speak to me of the hours of today;
> Don't speak to me of the past. . . .

Marian Russell tightened her grip on my hand as the man at the wheel twisted it sharply, and we turned off the road onto what seemed to be no more than a narrow path. We seemed to be driving through a forest. I could smell the pines in the cool night air. The singer's voice rose in sentimental agony.

"Turn it off!" I told him. "That can't be making her head feel any better."

For a moment I thought that he meant to ignore my demand, and I sensed why. Something about the course of her questions had threatened him. Obviously he did not want her to know who he was. But why?

Leaning over, he switched off the music, and at the same time we came out from under the trees. I could see a few pinpricks of light below us to the right. The headlights picked up stone-terraced land on either side of us, and I knew that we were driving through a vineyard.

"Are we there?" I asked him.

He did not answer me, and I realized that we were crossing a small wooden bridge. Over the sound of the motor I could hear the rush of water. Suddenly the horn blared, and in response a hundred lights seemed to flash on. There was a heavy iron gate in front of us. We approached it with undiminished speed, and it was thrown open minutes before we reached it. There was the skid of gravel under the wheels, and the smell of pines was replaced by the thick scent of mimosa. The lights lay directly before us, and through the shadows that they cast I could see a large stone house looming into the night.

"He knew the signal," the woman beside me cried. "Who is he? Why won't you tell me who he is?"

"I'm David," the young man said in a low voice as the car came to a stop in front of brilliantly illuminated stone steps that led to a thick oak door set deep into the stone. "You may as well know now."

"Oh, God!" Marian Russell mourned, swaying against me. "I've always been afraid that this would happen."

"You don't have to worry," David Ashor said in a hard voice, his back still against us. "I'll leave tomorrow. I've always known how difficult it was for you to accept the fact that you have a son."

CHAPTER

2

In the morning the shrieking of the peacocks woke me. I got out of bed and went to the open window to look out at them, only to find one of the great birds sitting on the ledge outside my window. Startled, I drew back and pulled the window down. The peacock began pecking at the panes with its beak, and then, after staring at me arrogantly with beady eyes, he turned and walked to the outer ledge, spreading his tail as he went, until the window was checkered with scarlet and indigo.

When he flew off, I saw that the garden below my window was filled with peacocks. Thirty or forty of them paraded up and down the stone paths that led between unkempt flower beds in which wild poppies struggled with golden gorse under vast trunk-entangled camellia trees, unclipped and overgrown with thick red flowers. The birds swept along like royalty, their long tails sweeping the ground, their blue breasts puffed. On the top of the stone wall that enclosed the garden a peacock stood alone, his tail fully spread. His discordant cry shattered the morning silence.

It was a beautiful morning. The rich green of the giant pines that stood beyond the wall was touched with gold, and when the window had been open, I had smelled the perfume of sun-ripened air. I glanced at my watch and found that it was nearly ten. Usually I did not like to sleep that late but last night when I had finally gone to bed, I had known that it would be by far the best thing if I slept until I awoke naturally.

I turned away from the window and looked about the room. The night before I had been too exhausted to notice details. It was a comfortable room, but with something strangely reminiscent of pictures I had seen of 1920 drawing rooms. There was no particular style. The walls were white-paneled, the inset portions etched with gold, a touch of French Provincial which should have had a brightening effect but somehow made me feel that I was standing inside an overelaborately decorated box. There were two paintings on the walls, one a Watteau-like genre landscape by Pierra Quillard, the other a view of the city of Oporto by Quillard's eighteenth-century contemporary, José Carvalho. The furniture was in odd contrast to the room itself. A vast canopied bed—a monstrous affair with dusty green-velvet hangings pulled back with gold cords to disclose massive oak bedposts and an elaborately carved headboard—dominated one-half of the bedroom. Black-walnut chairs with straight backs were set formally at regular intervals along the walls, and a walnut vanity table lurked beneath a mirror that was so large there was scarcely a place in the room where one could escape its reflection. Last night I had felt as though the room was crowded with all the people who had slept in it in the past. Even with the bright morning light flooding through the windows, I felt as though I had somehow intruded.

There was something hostile, as far as that went, about the house itself. I had been aware of it as soon as I had followed David Ashor through the doorway the night before. A single servant had greeted us, an old man wearing a dull black suit. He had approached us across the black-and-white-tiled floor of the vast hall, his shoulders bent, his gait a shuffle. His faded black eyes, set in a plump face as wizened as a newborn infant's, had fastened on us as suspiciously as though we were all strangers. I would never have taken him for Portuguese, but it was with a shock that I heard the Scottish burr in his voice.

David had lifted Marian Russell out of the car despite her feeble protests, and he brushed past the old man with no explanation of what had happened.

"What room is she in, MacGregor?" he had demanded. Marian's eyes were closed, and it was impossible to tell whether she was unconscious again, or was simply blotting out the sight of the man who had called himself her son. David started up the broad, winding stairs that led up to a sort of balcony.

"What room?" he demanded when the old man did not answer immediately.

"The yellow room," the servant muttered sullenly. "We've not been expecting you," he added resentfully.

"We'll need Senhora," David said. As he reached a bend in the stairs, I saw his face set in angry lines. "Fetch her at once. And another thing: There's no need to bother my aunt about this tonight. Do you hear?"

Muttering something under his breath, the old man shuffled through a door at the far end of the hall, leaving me alone. Uncertain as to whether I should follow David or not, I stood where I was and wearily looked around me. The hall was lighted by a baroque glass chandelier that hung on a thick gold chain from a ceiling two stories overhead. The ceiling itself caused me to catch my breath. It had been painted in the style of Tiepolo. Angels and

allegorical figures seemed to dart at me from among
delicately etched white clouds, which appeared to drift
against a background of vivid indigo. It was one of the
most superb ceiling paintings I had ever seen, and to find
it so unexpectedly looming over me was disconcerting.

I was still looking up at it when I heard the sound of
steps on the tiled floor. A woman was coming toward
me. Black eyes glittered in a broad, strong-boned Celtic
face. Her coarse black hair was pulled into a tight bun,
which seemed to strain at the skin of her forehead. She
might have been any age. Her body, thick as a peasant
woman's, was encased in a tweed skirt and a blue sweater.
But if her dress was that of an English country woman,
there was nothing British about the thickness of her accent, which was purely Portuguese.

"I am Senhora Sequeira," she said. Her mouth, set in a
thin line, scarcely moved when she spoke. There was
nothing of welcome in her attitude. "And you?"

"I'm Irene Haverlock," I said, aware of a rising anger.
"I believe I was expected today."

She made no response to that. "What has happened to
Miss Russell?" she demanded. "And why is Lady Stewart's
nephew here? You must understand that the situation
cannot be tolerated."

"I'm afraid that's no concern of mine," I said sharply.
"As for Miss Russell, there was an accident. She appears
to have suffered a concussion. Mr. Ashor has taken her
upstairs to her room. She needs a doctor—or a nurse.
Mr. Ashor said that Lady Stewart's companion is qualified
to examine her."

"I am Lady Stewart's companion," the dark woman
said, her deep voice tinged with sarcasm. "I assumed you
would realize that."

Her deliberate rudeness infuriated me. "I see no reason
why I should assume anything," I said sharply, "but if
you are who you say you are, I think that you ought to
go up to Miss Russell at once. And I would appreciate it

if you would see that someone brings my luggage in from the car."

"You won't be able to see Lady Stewart tonight," her companion said with a certain grim satisfaction.

"I have no intention of seeing anyone," I told her. "I want, however, to be shown my room and to have some food sent up to me. I left London at two this morning, and I have been traveling on incredible roads for the past four hours. I want to eat and to sleep—in that order, and at once."

For the first time the woman smiled. It was not a pleasant smile. "I told Lady Stewart that she should not bring strangers here," she said smugly. "It's quite clear that you will never do."

"That is for your employer to decide," I snapped. "Did you hear anything that I just said?"

The smile faded. "MacGregor will see to you," she said. "As you so kindly advised me, I must attend to Lady Stewart's niece. And if David is here, there will be other complications as well."

MacGregor must have been listening to us, for as soon as Senhora Sequeira had ascended the stairs, he appeared with a young brown-faced boy, and between them my luggage and myself were deposited in a bedroom on the second story. The old man made no response except to nod his head when I reiterated my request for food. I did not adopt the same tone with him that I had with Lady Stewart's companion, but I was firm. Through a daze of weariness I was certain of only one thing—and that was that I establish at once the basis on which I demanded to be treated.

Adjoining the bedroom was an old-fashioned bathroom, with the toilet perched high on a raised platform and a tub so deep and long that I could not recline in it with any degree of safety. Still, the water was hot, and there was a thick bar of lemon-scented soap and bath salts. Lulled by the warmth of the water, I tried to put everything that had happened into some sort of perspective and found that I could not. I had not particularly cared for Marian Russell, but my overriding emotion was one of anxiety about her condition. In a sense I felt that I should be with her, but despite Senhora Sequeira's rudeness, I had sensed in her a basic competence. If a doctor was needed, she would call one. It was difficult to think she would welcome any intrusion on my part. I only hoped that before I fell asleep, someone would come to tell me how the injured woman was.

But they did not. While I was toweling myself, a sullen-faced girl in a black uniform appeared, without knocking, in the bedroom and set a tray on the table beside the bed. The meal was light but delicious: thin slices of cold roast lamb, a bun and butter, a small salad covered with a white dressing I had never tasted before, and a bit of pale-yellow, tart-tasting cheese. There were two small carafes of wine, one a sparkling rosé and the other a rich, mellow port. I drank only one glass of the port after I had finished my meal, savoring the rich, mellow taste and remembering what my father had often told me about Douro port being the finest in the world. Scarcely able to hold my eyes open, I had fallen into the huge canopied bed and slept.

Now I realized, however, that only exhaustion and the wine had made my first hours at Alcombra relatively simple to face. Quickly bathing and brushing my hair, I slipped into a pair of white-linen slacks and a blue-jersey tunic. If I was going to begin work at once, I might as well be comfortable. But first, I supposed, must come an interview with Lady Stewart. I did not find the thought reassuring and lingered for a while in front of the huge mirror, pretending to deliberate as to whether I should rub some color into cheeks that seemed unnaturally pale, whether I should leave my hair hanging straight about my shoulders or pull it back in a loose bun. I decided on the

latter. I was twenty-six, but something about the sunlight
or the mirror or the fact that I was completely rested
made me look like a towheaded girl. I did not want Lady
Stewart to lose confidence in me at first sight.

I was about to open the door when someone knocked.
Senhora Sequeira stood outside in the shadows of the
cavernous corridor. Before I could speak, she stepped
inside the bedroom. The sullen-faced girl who had brought
my supper the night before was behind her, carrying another tray, covered with a white napkin. Without as
much as glancing at me, she placed it on the table by the
window and left the room, closing the door behind her.

I found that the unpleasantness of the night before made
it difficult for me to know what to say to the dark-faced
woman who stood stolidly before me, wearing the same
skirt and sweater she had worn when I had first seen her.
There were gray circles under her dark eyes, and her hair
was loosened about her face. There was something softer
about her appearance this morning. Although she did not
speak, she seemed more approachable. I hazarded a smile,
which she did not return.

"I was about to come to find you," I began. "I thought
that I ought to talk to Lady Stewart as soon as possible
so that I can begin my inventory. I know that she is
eager to have it completed as soon as possible."

"You must eat your breakfast first," Senhora said. "It
has been especially prepared for you, which is something
that is not usually done. You will find that we have a very
regular routine, Miss Haverlock. Breakfast is served in the
dining room promptly at nine. Guests are expected to eat
there if they wish to eat at all."

There was something about this woman that reminded
me of a headmistress I had particularly loathed. Under
ordinary circumstances I would have apologized for over-
sleeping, but I had no intention of ever apologizing to
Senhora Sequeira.

"Besides," she added when I made no response, "it will be a half hour at least before you can be interviewed by Lady Stewart."

She had, I knew, chosen the word "interviewed" especially to annoy me. Turning my back on her, I drew up a chair to the table near the window and flicked the napkin off the tray. She followed me and stood staring down at me, her arms folded across her thick breasts. In the full glare of the sunlight I could see that she looked incredibly tired. Suddenly I relented.

"Sit down and have some coffee," I said, making my voice as firm as hers had been. "You can have this cup. I only want juice and toast."

For a moment I thought that she would refuse, and then, her shoulders slumping, she drew up one of the black-walnut chairs and sat down across the table from me.

"Now," I said, pouring coffee from the ornate silver pot, "tell me about Miss Russell. Is she going to be all right?"

"It was not necessary to send for a doctor," the woman replied stiffly. "I examined her and found no signs of concussion or any other injury. I took the precaution, however, of staying with her through the night. When she awoke this morning, she seemed to be her usual self. There is no need to tell Lady Stewart of the incident. I wish to make that quite clear. Her doctor has impressed on me the need for her to be undisturbed by . . . minor problems."

There was an absurd note of authority in her voice, and for a moment I was angry again. But then I noticed that the hand that held the coffee cup was unsteady. For some reason this woman was not as assured as she wished to sound. I did not believe that she had come to me simply to warn me not to tell Lady Stewart about the accident, and if she did in fact have another reason, I intended to find out what it was, even if it meant controlling my temper.

I waited for her to go on, but when she did not, I asked her about David. "Has he gone yet?" I said. "He said last night that he was leaving this morning."

The woman's dark eyes narrowed. For a moment she did not answer, and then, clicking the coffee cup against the saucer, she said: "Lady Stewart has already seen him this morning. She will not hear of his leaving so abruptly. If anyone is to go, it must be his mother."

I drew in my breath. Somehow I had never quite believed what David had implied the night before when he had said that he had always known that she found it difficult to accept the fact that she had a son. It had seemed too incredible to be true when, up to that point, neither of them had given any sign of recognition.

"Then it's true?" I said. "Miss Russell *is* his mother?"

Senhora stared at me suspiciously. "I thought you were aware of that," she said. "I would never have spoken otherwise."

"David said something about it last night," I told her, "and yet when he first came across us on the mountain, just after the accident, he didn't appear to recognize her."

"There is no reason why he should," Senhora said in a tight voice, "since neither have set eyes on the other since he was a child in arms."

I stared at her incredulously. "She gave him up?" I said. "But why?"

"It is an old story," the woman said, "and like most old stories, better forgotten. Besides, you will understand me when I remind you that it is purely a family affair."

She had a masterful use of the barb. Obviously she saw herself as some sort of protector of Lady Stewart and, if necessary, of the entire family. She had told me enough to make me curious and then verbally slapped my hands for asking questions. If I had not sensed a certain viciousness about her, I would have been amused.

"But why is his name Ashor?" I insisted. "That wouldn't be a very intimate detail to divulge, would it?"

She did not take well to being mocked, even gently. Pushing her cup away from her, she rose. "David has taken his father's name," she said. "I answer these questions because I do not wish you to impose them on Lady Stewart. You will be in this house only a few weeks, Miss Haverlock. It is unfortunate, perhaps, that certain members of the family will be here at the same time, but I can see no reason why you should concern yourself either with them personally or with their affairs."

I rose, facing her. "And is that what you came to tell me?" I said in a low voice.

"I came to warn you, Miss Haverlock," Senhora said, her eyes flashing. "I guessed last night that you might be the sort to interfere, and I warn you: If you do, I will see to it that you leave Alcombra."

"Don't argue with me, Senhora," Lady Stewart said. "I won't stand for it. Do you understand? I won't stand for it."

Clutching the cane that leaned against the bed, she cracked it sharply across the legs of a small mahogany table, overturning a glass of water, which deluged a tray on which bottles of pills stood in neatly ordered lines. For a long moment the two women stared at one another with undisguised loathing, the one propped massively against lace-edged pillows in a high bed canopied with faded blue-velvet hangings on which the dust stood out like a frosting of snow, the other standing straight against the oak-paneled wall, her dark face scarcely visible in the shadows. Thick drapes were pulled across the windows, shutting out the day. The only light came from a small lamp beside the bed.

Lady Stewart turned her head against the pillows and stared down at me. My chair was lower than the bed, and the old woman's thick, hawk-nosed face seemed to jut, neckless, from rounded shoulders wrapped in a plaid shawl. Her black eyes darted from my face to that of her companion and back again.

"Since I've been ill," she said in a deep voice, "Senhora has seen fit to treat me as though I had lost my mind. On the whole, of course, that's more acceptable than the attitude my relatives have taken. I find it singularly disconcerting to have it assumed that since I am dying, I might as well be dead. Once you have met them, Miss Haverlock, you will understand what I mean. They wing about like vultures."

It was easy to see from whom Senhora had taken lessons in abruptness. Strangely enough, however, as soon as she had led me into the shadowy bedroom, she had seemed to shrink—to diminish in some way. Outside of this room she was obviously a power, but here she paled into insignificance beside the old woman, who seemed to rear out of the bed.

"Senhora Sequeira has been my companion for nearly thirty years," Lady Stewart said. "She has many excellent qualities, but she is inclined to be overly secretive. She has never learned to admire truth as I do." With an obvious effort, she pulled herself away from the pillows, gripping the edge of the bed with a hand that could have been a man's. "She doesn't want me to talk about my personal affairs now, do you, Senhora? You consider garrulity one of my many weaknesses, don't you?"

"What you talk about is your own affair, your ladyship."

"Quite right!" the old woman crowed triumphantly. "It *is* my own affair. And now will you tell me why you persist in hiding in the shadows? Come here."

It was a command, made deliberately as a show of strength. As long as an order was obeyed, there could be no doubt about where power lay. I guessed that the old woman was reminding the younger of that. Perhaps there was a message there for me as well. I watched the dark, tight-faced woman move out of the shadows and into the pool of light which encircled the old woman in the bed and myself.

Lady Stewart's eyes flickered over the companion as though she were presenting a particularly uninteresting exhibit. "I do not want you to misunderstand, Miss Haverlock," she said in a mocking voice. "Senhora is indispensable to me. She knows my ways. There will be times when my orders to you will be conveyed through her. But they will always be *my* orders, won't they, Senhora? Always *my* orders."

Her companion nodded, her dark eyes fixed on the blankets that bulked themselves over the old woman's body. I noticed that her hands were clenched.

"Senhora has always been afraid that someone new would usurp, as it were, her particular functions," Lady Stewart explained, a malicious smile twisting her lips. "I attempted to make it clear to her when I arranged for you to come here that your duties would be well defined. You are to catalog my possessions—nothing more."

"That was my understanding," I said. I had been in the room for no more than ten minutes, but I wanted nothing more than to leave it. The oil portraits that lined the oak-paneled walls oppressed me with their sightless eyes, and the air seemed to be heavy with the smell of dead and dying things.

"It wasn't necessary for you to bring in a stranger," the dark-skinned woman said suddenly in a loud, defiant voice. "I could have done everything that needs to be done. It's simply a matter of making lists."

Lady Stewart's laugh came from deep in her throat as she fell back against the pillows. There was something of a man about her, even discounting the thickness of her features and the way in which her white hair was cropped. Although I guessed that the bottom part of her body was lifeless, there was a restless vitality about her, a forcefulness that demanded attention.

"*You* see to everything?" she said scornfully. "You're
a fool, Senhora, even to consider it. You don't know the
difference between a Goya and a Velázquez, let alone a
Patini and a Perugino. Miss Haverlock is an expert, or so
I have been led to believe. She can do what needs to
be done quickly, and time is of the essence. The doctor
explained all that to you, didn't he, Senhora? As a nurse
you shouldn't find it too difficult to understand what is
happening to me."

"The doctor can't possibly be certain," her companion
muttered.

"He knows all he needs to know about death," the old
woman insisted, almost gleefully. "I have six weeks at
the most. Let Miss Haverlock look after the collection.
If you want to keep busy, you can plan the funeral." She
laughed again.

"Don't!" her companion said harshly. "It's not good
for you to upset yourself."

The old woman's face settled into heavy lines. "If I
can't talk about my own death, who can?" she asked.
"The point is, there has to be an inventory, or the be-
reaved will be off with all they can carry before I'm
cold. Do you think you can get the job done in six
weeks, Miss Haverlock?"

"I haven't seen the collection yet," I said. "I hadn't
intended to spend longer than three weeks at the most."

"You see, Senhora," Lady Stewart said in a pleased
voice. "This young woman knows what she has to do, and
she wants to get on with it without any beating around
the bush. She doesn't want to become involved with us and
our quibbling. She's not even particularly impressed by
the fact that I'm dying. It should be an object lesson to
you, Senhora. You are inclined to take life much too
personally yourself."

If she hoped to disconcert me, she was mistaken. I kept
my face expressionless, but Senhora Sequeira flushed and

seemed somehow, without moving, to falter. The old woman obviously knew by heart all the ways she could hurt her. Grinning, Lady Stewart pushed herself higher on her pillows, her face suddenly becoming a mask of pain. Senhora bent over her to help her, but the old woman pushed her away.

"Of course," she said to me, her voice weaker, "I may have less than six weeks—or more. These doctors don't know as much as they pretend. I may 'linger on,' as they say, longer than expected. That would be a nice state of affairs, wouldn't it, Senhora?"

"Don't talk like that," the dark woman said harshly, her dark eyes riveted on Lady Stewart's face.

"Does it really upset you to think of me dead?" the old woman said quizzically. "I can't think why it should, really. You'll be well provided for—not a rich woman, of course. You won't be able to live as you've been accustomed to living for the past thirty years. And you have developed a certain taste for luxury over the years, haven't you, Senhora?"

Shoulders stiff, her companion turned and hurried out of the room. I rose to follow her.

"No," Lady Stewart said impatiently, "I want to talk to you alone, Miss Haverlock. That was just my way of getting Senhora to leave the room. She never would have done so while you were here otherwise. I expect our little games don't make much sense to you, do they?"

"There's no reason why they should," I said sharply. I loathed these kind of female involutions, and I saw no need to pretend otherwise.

The old woman closed her eyes. It was as though someone had drawn a curtain. The forcefulness, the strength, the vitality—all disappeared. For the first time I realized that she was suffering. Her voice, when she spoke, seemed to come from a great distance.

"You're annoyed, aren't you?" she said.

"Perhaps," I said, "we ought to discuss where you want me to begin."

"Later!" Her eyes snapped open like a turtle's. "Tell me, what have you heard about me?"

I met her eyes. "That you're a well-known collector of art. That you have one of the largest private collections in the world."

"Yes, yes." Her thick, mannish face stiffened with impatience. "But what have you heard about me as a human being?"

I hesitated. "I've heard that you have a reputation for eccentricity," I said slowly.

"And what did you take that to mean?"

"That you go your own way, make your own rules."

"But not that I'm insane?"

It was not a casual question. Her voice burned with intensity. She lay motionless against the pillows, her gnarled hands clutching at the plaid shawl, but somehow she conveyed the sense of movement. She might have been pacing back and forth in front of me.

"No," I said, "I've never heard that."

Again she pushed a laugh from the back of her throat. "And what do you think now?" she asked. "Now that you've seen me?"

"I think that you're a very forceful person," I told her. "Very strong. You like to dominate other people."

"But I'm sane? You believe that I'm sane?"

I was suddenly aware of a feeling of exhaustion. "Of course," I said.

"Others aren't so certain," she muttered, "or perhaps they simply believe what they want to believe. I spoke of vultures a moment ago. You ought to know that by that I meant my family: my stepson, my niece, the lot of them. For a long time I've managed to stay clear of them. Now I can't even keep them out of this room, let alone out of the house. You'll meet them soon enough."

She paused and took a deep breath that was something between a gasp and a sigh. For the first time I realized that it was an effort for her to speak, but that she would not face the fact that she could no longer sustain her enormous vitality.

"I only mention them because you ought to know that all of them are opposed to your being here." She reached out and grasped her cane, pounding it against the floor as though she were afraid that she was losing my attention. "Do you understand what I'm talking about?"

I knew that it would be a kindness to her to pretend that I did, to leave her alone to rest. And yet, although I had lied a good deal at one time or other in my life, I found it impossible to meet those blazing black eyes and circumvent the truth simultaneously.

"I'm afraid I don't," I said, "but perhaps it would be better if you explained tomorrow."

"It would not be better!" the old woman said. "By tomorrow they will have gotten to you. You have to know that every one of them is opposed to my turning this place into a museum. That's what they're here for: to persuade me to change my mind before it's too late. The fools! I've spent my life collecting things of value for this purpose. The money was mine to spend. My husband left it to me because he knew that I was the only one of the lot that would put it to good use, and now they want to turn it into cold cash again—sell everything, divide the money. They're willing to go to any length. They'll try to prove that I'm not in my right mind if they have to. This inventory. . . ."

She broke off, gasping for breath. The cane fell from her hand to the floor. Rising, I went to the bed. The gnarled hand clutched my arm and pulled me down until my face was close to hers.

"Senhora!" She could scarcely choke out the words. "Call Senhora! She shouldn't have left me, no matter what

I said. But she's like the others. They hate me, all of them. They've been waiting for me to die for a long time."

When Lady Stewart was a girl, her portrait had been painted by Sargent. It hung now at the end of the long gallery that stretched the entire length of the wing where the major portion of the collection was evidently housed. I approached it slowly, scarcely noticing the other paintings on either side. The artist had painted her as she turned away from him. Her pale-golden hair was pulled back in an elegant chignon from her delicate, fine-boned face. She was smiling enigmatically, and her eyes sparkled as though something the artist had said had amused her. Her slender body was draped in a white evening gown, which swirled about her feet and left her translucent shoulders bare. It was incredible to think that this beautiful girl could have been transformed by time into the mottle-faced old woman I had just seen gasping for breath against her pillows.

It had not been necessary for me to ring for Senhora. She had come stalking into the room nearly as soon as Lady Stewart had called her name, and I assumed that she must have been listening outside the door. I had left her administering an injection into the old woman's arm. Since then I had been roaming this wing of the house with growing incredulity.

The sheer extent of the collection left me breathless. I had passed through five rooms before coming to this gallery, which formed the L of the wing, and each room had been crammed with objects of art, each wall thick with paintings. It was difficult to examine anything closely because of the poor quality of the lighting. The windows, which were set high in the oak-paneled walls, cut out more daylight than they admitted, ornamented as they were with iron fretwork, each with its own elaborate pattern of Moorish floral designs. Artificial lighting was restricted to wall lamps in the form of three-pronged candelabra supporting tiny flamelike bulbs that did little to illuminate even the largest canvases.

Each one of the five rooms was large and high-vaulted, with timbered ceilings on which painted panels were dimly visible. Hooded fireplaces jutted from the walls, and the floors were covered with beautiful glistening black tiles, genuine Moorish tile with a purplish cast. These tiles, called *azulejos,* were, I knew, common in Portugal. One found them in all colors—blue and yellow and green and pink—decorating the facades of houses and lining the inner walls of churches. The black tiles were rare, however, and I had never before seen them used as a floor covering. The moment I stepped into the first of these rooms I realized that what I was about to see was more amazing by far than anything rumor had prepared me to expect.

The rooms were furnished with antiques, which took the chill off what might otherwise have been a complete museum atmosphere, but it was difficult to imagine people sitting in the high wing chairs upholstered in faded tapestry. Long refectory tables—handsome, massive pieces, with lion-clawed legs—were set in the center of each room. Escritoires were dotted about in odd corners, but it was clear that it had been many years since anyone had penned a letter on their dusty tops. There were flat-topped glass tables everywhere, their surfaces covered with green felt. Various mementos, including letters, rested beneath the surfaces of the glass, but the light was too dim for me to see exactly what was there. It was clear that I would need some more adequate source of light before I could begin any sort of inventory.

One room had proved an exception to the general rule. Just before I had reached the long gallery, I had passed through a small chapel that appeared to have been transported piece by piece from an eleventh-century Romanesque church, with horseshoe arches and a delightful pregnant Madonna standing by the low altar. There were two arched windows set with brilliantly colored medieval glass, one portraying the Pentecost and the other an Annunciation scene. On the altar itself I found a doll-like figure of Jesus as a young boy, dressed incongruously in a black frock coat and knee breeches. On hooks beside him hung other costumes that I knew had been made, according to time-honored custom, by peasant women who had stitched each garment with piety to show their affection for their Lord. But perhaps the most surprising thing the chapel contained was a small stone tomb on which the alabaster figure of a young boy dressed in fifteenth-century costume lay sleeping. The effigy was so realistically carved that I had found myself brushing my hand over the sleeve that partially covered one delicately wrought hand as though to push back the cloth.

Nothing I had seen, however, had prepared me for the long gallery with the portrait by Sargent at the far end. Turning away from the beauty that had been Lady Stewart's when she was a girl, I stood on tiptoe to examine the other paintings, finding a treasure trove of sixteenth-century Portuguese art: brilliant group scenes by Gonçalves, showing the influence of the Flemish masters of the period; biblical scenes by Henriques, with their incredible clarity; and the static faces of Fernandes. For the first time since I had come here, I felt a sense of great excitement. Even if the inventory took me more than three weeks to finish—and it seemed clear that it would—it would be an experience that could not be duplicated. The tensions I had encountered here, the hatred, no longer seemed to matter. I would isolate myself as much as I could from the other people gathered in this house and concentrate on this extraordinary collection.

There was a narrow door set deep in the wall to my right, and I opened it, expecting to find myself in still another room, only to emerge into the glare of full sunlight. I was standing in a courtyard apparently formed by the wing I had been exploring on my right and the main house on the left. A cloistered walk, which must have once graced a monastery, ran along the two sides of the wing, and beyond the graceful columned arches was the court-yard itself, laid out in formal gardens through which ran gravel paths. Shade was provided by orange trees, their glossy dark leaves shielding the red-gold fruit. In the cen-ter of the garden stood the stone sculpture of a pig, ap-parently a smaller replica of the famous Pig of Murça. Crudely carved, its bestial quality struck an ominous note amid so much beauty.

"It's even more vicious looking than the Pig of Bragança, don't you agree?" a man's voice said.

Turning, I saw him coming across the grass, a tall, slender, dark-haired man, with a narrow, sharply boned face and dark eyes that were half veiled by oddly drooping lids. His skin was olive in color, and there was no more doubt than there had been about Senhora that he was Portuguese. But it was equally obvious that he was not a servant. His clothing was expensive and fashionable. His trousers were narrow and beautifully tapered, and his high-cut calfskin boots were glossed with a rich shine. Over a brown high-necked jersey he wore a tan thickly knit sweater, which was belted about the waist. Yet despite the foppishness of his dress, there was an enormous virility about the man. From a distance I had guessed that he was not much older than David, but now that he approached me and the statue, I saw that he must be in his forties.

"It's amazing how many of these artifacts you'll find scattered around this country," he went on. There was only the slightest trace of accent in his voice. "Any size at all. It's possible that the pig was worshiped in pre-historic times, of course—quite clearly possible. After all, primitive man frequently makes a deity out of any animal on which he depends for his livelihood. And the number of chestnut trees—particularly in Bragança, of course—

means that there was always plenty of forage for pigs. And we know that the pig's fat was used for soups and also for lamp oil, not to mention the meat itself."

Reaching past me, he stroked the granite side of the stone beast and looked directly at me for the first time, smiling.

"You must excuse me for not introducing myself at once," he said. "I am Jerez Caravels, Marian's fiancé. Probably she mentioned me to you during your long drive together yesterday. I was very much opposed to her making the trip to fetch you alone, you understand. Portugal's roads are a great deal better than they were a few years ago, but the mountain roads are still treacherous. And then, of course, there is Marian's driving to consider. She's quite competent, of course—I don't mean that—but she knows nothing about the machine itself, which is, I think, always a mistake. One would not qualify as an adequate horseman if one knew nothing about the beast itself. However, I might as well have kept my arguments to myself. She insisted on going alone." He made a wide expansive gesture, white teeth glittering as he laughed. "She said that she wanted to talk to you—alone."

I stared at him, bewildered. He had come upon me out of nowhere, obviously knowing who I was, and begun to talk as though we were intimate friends. What he had said about stone pigs and Marian jumbled together in my mind.

"And did she?" he asked.

"Did she what?"

"Talk to you."

Something about his confidence that I would respond openly to him irritated me. "Of course we talked," I said sharply. "One rarely travels that distance with someone else without exchanging some conversation."

"Ah, you are very much what I expected you to be, Miss Haverlock!" He ran his fingers lightly over the flank of the stone pig. The smile remained set on his face.

"Very practical, very businesslike, very English. A great deal younger than I had imagined, of course. And I had not even considered the possibility that you might be beautiful."

"How is Marian this morning?" I said stiffly.

He shrugged. "I am told that she is nearly recovered, but Senhora is seeing that she is guarded as closely as is the old woman. There is one way only to Senhora's heart, and that is illness, disaster, or catastrophe. Under ordinary circumstances she prefers to pretend that Marian does not exist. Last night she guarded her as jealously as a dragon guards a princess." He laughed and took my arm. "Forgive me for my awkward metaphors, Miss Haverlock," he said. "It is possible to envision Senhora as a dragon, but with all due respect to Marian, princess is not part of her image."

He was guiding me down one of the gravel paths away from the stone pig, toward the main house, as though we had a common destination. I wanted to pull my arm away to prove, if for no other reason, that I was not the sort of woman he could charm so easily. But I sensed that if I did so, I would only succeed in appearing gauche.

"No doubt you find me hopelessly garrulous," he was saying as he bent and picked a spray of mimosa and handed it to me, "but I am a man who likes the company of others, and without Marian around, this place is like a morgue. Worse. In a morgue people can talk freely. The dead will not be disturbed. But here. . . . Have you seen Lady Stewart?"

"I talked with her for a while this morning."

"How did she impress you?" Dropping my arm, he moved in front of me and stopped, blocking my path.

"She is an extraordinary person," I said slowly. Why was it that I should feel that everyone in this house wanted something from me? I knew before he told me that that was not the kind of impression he had wanted described.

"Ah, yes. She is certainly extraordinary. A woman with a vision is always extraordinary. Visions are the property of *men* under ordinary circumstances. There have been few Joan of Arcs, and that is, I think, a very good thing."

For the first time since we had met, he amused me. His mind was like a magpie's nest—or seemed to be. I had met women before who had flitted from the top of one topic to that of another but never a man. It occurred to me that this man might be being flip deliberately to put me off my guard—although that was absurd, of course. This was probably his normal manner toward attractive women. I had been only a few hours in this house, and already I was becoming paranoid. What could be more natural than that this man should want to know my impressions of Lady Stewart?

"I expect," he went on, taking my arm again and continuing our promenade down the gravel path, "that Marian told you yesterday her opinion of her aunt's idea to establish a museum here at Alcombra."

I avoided the question. "From what I've seen this morning," I said, "Lady Stewart has a collection that would do justice to a museum. Does she intend to leave the house and the contents to the care of the state?"

"No. No." Jerez Caravels was no longer smiling. "That is not her way, as you will discover, no doubt. A trust is to be established. The museum is to be privately operated and maintained. There will be no admission fee. An admirable idea, no doubt, although I find that no one else agrees with me. I expect you to help me convince them, Miss Haverlock, that Lady Stewart could do nothing better with her fortune than to leave the fruits of it to posterity. That phrase is not mine. The old woman is particularly fond of referring to posterity. One would think that the future was her own invention."

He broke off as there a rushing noise in the flowers, and a great white peacock dashed away from us, emitting shrill screams of apparent outrage at having been disturbed. Involuntarily I found myself clutching the arm of the man beside me.

"Those peacocks are a nuisance," Jerez said blandly. "There must be over a hundred of them on the grounds. They'll overrun the place in time. As soon as the old woman's dead, at least half of them should be destroyed, but it won't happen. She's taken care of that in her will, I understand—the famous will. From what I hear, she's taken care that everything will go on here just as though she were still alive. It's her way of guaranteeing her own immortality. I've tried to explain all that to Marian, but she doesn't want to accept it. Perhaps you can make her see that there's nothing she can do to change things."

We had reached the shadows of the main house. It rose above us, the whitewashed walls glittering in the sunlight. I paused and looked back across the courtyard, past the hulking statue of the prehistoric pig. Beyond lay the cool cloisters that lined the wing where the collection was housed. I was aware of a sudden intense desire to hide myself away in those dusky rooms, to escape once and for all the insistence of these strangers that I involve myself in their personal affairs.

"I might as well tell you, Mr. Caravels," I said slowly, "that I have no intention of explaining anything to anyone. I'm here for only one reason: to make an inventory. As soon as that is finished, I intend to return to England."

For a moment he looked at me intently. There was something disconcerting about his heavy-lidded stare. "You find the personal affairs of strangers of no interest?" he said slowly.

"Precisely," I said. "You've put it very well. I'm aware that there are certain tensions——"

"Has anyone ever told you that you are a master of understatement?"

The faintly teasing tone he insisted on taking with me was infuriating.

"You'll have to excuse me," I said. "I want to start work as soon as possible."

"But surely you can't intend to begin now," Jerez Caravels said lightly. "It's nearly time for lunch, and I can assure you after a three-week stay in this house that if you intend to eat at all, you must put in an appearance for the three formal meals of the day."

I remembered what Senhora had said about it not being customary for breakfast to be served in one's room and nodded. "I think that today at least I'll skip lunch," I said. "I'm rather eager to begin."

"You have your instructions from Lady Stewart?"

It was none of his concern, and I wanted to tell him so. But at the same time I wanted to avoid outright rudeness. I had been frank with him a moment before, but rudeness was quite another thing.

"No," I admitted. "When I saw her this morning, she was not feeling particularly well, but I don't think that that presents any difficulty. I know how to proceed."

"Still," Jerez said, smiling, "I think that you will make a mistake in not appearing for lunch."

"Why?" I demanded wearily. "I can't think of any conceivable reason why it should matter one way or the other."

"There are a number of excellent reasons," he told me. "You will pardon me if I insist on telling you about them. I have a certain empathy with you, whether or not you care to admit it. We are in much the same boat, you and I. Neither of us are related to Lady Stewart, nor do we have any vested interest in her affairs."

"I thought that you said that you were Marian Russell's fiancé," I said caustically.

He laughed. "I suppose that does give me a certain interest—or would if the will were a different one. But no one here is going to inherit anything, other than the small bequests that go to Senhora and MacGregor. I am here only because Marian insisted, but that is not the point.

We were speaking of the small matter of luncheon. If you have met Senhora, you realize that she is a touchy, difficult woman. And her influence in this house is great. She supervises everything, even the housekeeper. As a consequence Alcombra is run with a certain monotonous regularity, and when that regularity is not observed, there is the devil to pay. The table will be set for six—that is, if Marian is well enough to come down—and if six do not appear, there will be ripples in the pool. And I assure you, Miss Haverlock, we do not at present need more ripples in this particular pool."

I believed him, even though it sounded absurd that it could matter one way or another whether I turned up for lunch. I remembered the reverberations that had resulted from my failure to appear for breakfast and felt my heart quite literally sink.

Jerez glanced at his watch. "Now," he said, "we have precisely twenty minutes before we will be expected in the dining room. Sit down here in the shade and let me continue to prattle. You are a difficult woman to carry on a dialogue with, Miss Haverlock, and I find that rather refreshing. Monologues have always been my forte, as you may have guessed."

I did as he said. The wrought-iron bench was draped with honeysuckle. The scent was overpowering. I smiled. This man had ceased to irritate me. He had tried to amuse me, and he had finally succeeded. Not that that changed my intention to remain aloof. But he had tried to be helpful, I knew, and I understood that if I wanted to work uninterruptedly that afternoon, I might as well follow whatever routine had been established and give neither Senhora nor anyone else an excuse to interrupt me. Perhaps, over lunch, I could make it clear to all of them that I had a good deal to do and that I had to be left alone to do it. Perhaps I had been wrong to think that without making myself clear, I could hope for any peace.

"All right," I said. "Now I *will* ask a question. Who

will the six be? Yourself, of course. And me, apparently. And perhaps Miss Russell——"

"Marian!" he exclaimed, sitting down beside me and smoothing the crease in his trousers with finger and thumb. "For heaven's sake, don't attempt to be formal. You may think it will make things easier, but I assure you that it will not."

"All right. Marian, then. Who else will be there? Senhora?"

"Good Lord, she wouldn't think of violating the conventions by dining with us. Senhora was born and raised in Lisbon, but somewhere along the line she was really inoculated with some firm Victorian values. No, she eats with the housekeeper—if she eats. I'm not at all certain that she doesn't sustain herself on her own venom."

Our eyes met, and we burst out laughing. He had the caustic humor of a woman, and despite myself, I responded to it. Obviously he was delighted. I guessed that he took great pleasure in making women respond, but there did not seem to be anything deliberate in the way he went about it, and for that I was willing to forgive him a great deal.

"There's another reason in favor of your lunching with us," he said. "And that——"

"But you haven't told me who will be there," I persisted.

"Well, there will be David, of course. I understand that you've already met David. He. . . ." Jerez broke off as though unwilling to break the mood.

"The others?" I encouraged him. I, too, did not want to talk about David. I was willing to spend a few minutes in light gossip, but not, for some reason, about him.

"William Stewart and his wife," Jerez said slowly. "Lady Stewart's stepson."

I no longer felt amused. Suddenly I remembered the old woman's voice when she had spoken of the vultures gathering. Jerez began to speak more rapidly, as though he was aware that he had begun to lose my interest.

"He was a grown man when she married his father," he said. "He's in his fifties now. Claire, his wife, is young, very young. Beautiful and greedy. A common combination in women, unfortunately. They are an interesting couple. Neither of them will have anything to do with me, of course. They consider my—er—position a compromising one. As a matter of fact you will find that few of us sitting around the table have anything at all in common—except, of course, Alcombra and what it contains."

He laughed, deprecatingly. "I am forgetting what I intended to say," he said. "Which was simply that there is a second reason that you should lunch with us. William Stewart considers that everything here is his—despite the will. After all, as he is so fond of saying, all of the collection was purchased with his father's money. He is here . . . well, who knows why he is here? Although one can guess. But one reason is certainly that he wishes to keep his eye very closely on what is going on, and he will want to talk to you. I suspect that he will want to talk to you very seriously—perhaps more seriously than you would like."

Leaning toward me, he took my hand. His hooded eyes were intent on my face. "I suspect," he said in a low voice, "that you find me a bit of a fool, Miss Haverlock. But like myself, I think that you came here imagining that you could remain the observer, and so I feel that I must warn you that it would be dangerous for you not to see quite clearly what is going on around you."

CHAPTER

3

The dining room opened off the tiled hall where I had been left waiting the night before. In the small anteroom between the hall and the dining room itself Jerez pointed out a miniature wine cask on a low table beside which was set a tray of glasses and a crystal decanter full of a ruby-colored liquid.

"Port," Jerez said, "from grapes grown here at Alcombra. You knew that this is one of the great vineyards of the Oporto region, didn't you? You wouldn't be aware of it unless you walked about the estate, but it's there, I assure you: rich, terraced lands. Lady Stewart may have devoted herself to her art collection, but her husband loved this land. The wine tells you just how much he loved it. Here."

Tipping the decanter, he poured the rich scarlet liquid into two of the tiny glasses.

"Try this." He raised his glass to his lips. Coming

straight from the brilliance of the day outside, I could not see his face in the dusk of the anteroom, but I sensed that he was on edge. Outside in the courtyard he had rattled on unselfconsciously. Now there was an edge to his voice that I had not heard before.

"Cheers."

Our glasses touched, and we drank. Port is a heavy wine to drink before any meal, let alone lunch, but my father had told me once that even the English wine merchants in the Oporto region imbibed their native product at any time of the day or night. Here in this house I guessed that the tasting had become a custom, probably begun while Lady Stewart's husband was alive. The decanter and the cask from which it was kept filled was placed where they were to ensure that every guest would be given the chance to appreciate the product of a famous vineyard. I held the wine in my mouth, savoring the rich bouquet.

"And now," Jerez said, taking my glass from me, "prepare for the direct encounter, my dear Miss Haverlock, or if you don't mind, I'll call you Irene. The others are waiting for us."

The dining room was cool and dim and elegant, its deep-set arched windows filled with elaborate grillwork, the plastered ceilings decorated in fluted patterns. The floor tiles were of a pale-blue that created the liquid impression of shallow water. A long black-oak sideboard stood against one wall, and the dining table itself stretched like a slender black finger down the center of the room. Pale-yellow place mats set off the sparkling silver. Crystal goblets caught and bent the few flickering rays of sunlight that penetrated the grilled windows. A huge cluster of yellow roses were at the center of the table.

David was standing just inside the door, still dressed as he had been the night before, in stained white chinos and a bulky sweater. His face was pale, and his long blond hair was pushed back untidily from his high forehead.

He started toward me, smiling, and then, apparently seeing Jerez behind me, stood by the end of the table and nodded stiffly.

Beyond him was a man whom I identified as William Stewart. Thick-set, with graying hair cut flat across his forehead, he stared at me with small pinched eyes that were nearly lost in his broad-nosed, fleshy face. Beside him the young woman who must be Claire, his wife, was talking vivaciously with another man whose back was toward me. She glanced for a moment in my direction, and I caught sight of the perfect oval of her face before she turned back to continue her conversation, throwing back her neck and shaking her long blond hair over her shoulders. Marian Russell was not in the room.

I heard Jerez introducing me, and I suppose I made the appropriate response. But I could no longer notice details. The man Claire Stewart had been talking to had turned so that I could see him full face, and I caught my breath as I saw his incredible resemblance to Philip.

Somehow we were all being seated. David was pulling out my chair. He slumped into a seat beside me and fingered the goblet closest to him with long, restless fingers.

"I tried to find you this morning," he said. "I wanted to tell you that I'm sorry about last night. I know you'll find it difficult to believe, but I didn't know who—who she was until you said her name. I haven't seen her since I was old enough to remember."

I felt a sudden rush of relief that he had chosen to be as direct with me as he had been the night before. With the others, I did not want to hear even the most superficial truths that influenced their lives, but with David it was different. And there was more to it than that. I welcomed the respite of talking to him. The man to whom Claire Stewart had been talking was seated at the far end of the table. I needed an excuse not to look at him again.

"You must think we're an odd lot," David went on as

a dark-haired maid bent between us to put a fruit salad in front of me. "I'm glad I'm not you, trapped here for weeks."

He spoke in a low voice, although there was no need. William Stewart was talking in a loud booming voice to Jerez, although I could feel his eyes on me. Beside him his wife was still intent in conversation with the man whose name I had not caught, the man who so closely resembled Philip. Her voice was high and light, sweeping over her husband's like a thin breeze.

"I had heard that you were going to stay," I said.

David's thin face hardened. "Who told you that?" he asked.

For a moment silence swept the table, and then the talk began again, louder than before, Jerez leading with a rapid staccato of words.

I shrugged. The salad was delicious, but I found I had no appetite. I put down my spoon. "I can't remember," I said. "Senhora, perhaps, or your great-aunt."

"Lelia probably," David said, scowling. "She enjoys nothing better than making an impossible situation worse. She pretends to hate having her family around her, and in a way, I think she's being honest enough when she says that. But once they are here, she has to control them. It's as though she relishes pitting them against one another, watching them tear one another apart." He laughed. "I expect," he said, "I'm being overly dramatic."

His eyes flickered, and then he looked down at his plate. He had not, I noticed, eaten any more than I had. "It wouldn't hurt me to stay," he said, "but my. . . ."

I realized suddenly that he found it impossible to say the definitive word.

"Your mother," I murmured.

"Yes." Now it was his turn to shrug. "I don't think she can bear to tear herself away now. I mean, I stayed in her room last night until Senhora came. She was talking a good deal—not to me, just talking. Shock, perhaps. But from the few things I heard, I don't think she'll let anything drive her away from here just now—even me. And if I stay——"

"Miss Haverlock."

If the man across from me realized that he was interrupting, he gave no sign. Leaning against the table, William Stewart somehow managed to give the impression that now that he had turned his attention to me, no one else was in the room.

"Mr. Caravels has been telling me that you have had an opportunity to visit the collection," he continued portentously. "I would be very interested in your opinion."

"It's even more impressive than I imagined it would be," I said.

"Yes, yes!" His thick voice was impatient. "We all know about that. What I want to know is, do you think it's possible for one person to complete the inventory in time?"

The folds of fat on his face seemed to envelope his small eyes, making it difficult to look at him directly. I felt a wave of repugnance.

"What 'time' did you have in mind?" I asked coldly.

I heard Jerez chuckle.

"He means, Can you get it done before Lelia dies?" David drawled.

"I see no reason for you to refer to your great-aunt by her given name," the older man said sharply.

David shrugged. The second course was being served: croquettes *ameijpas*, which my father had loved and sought out in the few Portuguese restaurants in London. MacGregor had appeared, making a shuffling, slump-shouldered circuit of the table, pouring wine with a hand that trembled. If it had not been for the way in which his sharp, dark eyes darted from one face to another, I would have thought him oblivious to what was being said. Jerez held his wineglass in front of him as the old man poured, watching the sparkling liquid subside against the crystal.

"Bairrada," he said, letting the name of the wine slip between his lips slowly. His hooded eyes darted from me to David to William Stewart. It was obvious that he was deliberately providing a distraction. "Like champagne in appearance, don't you agree? But the bouquet is quite different. It's a gayer wine. At least I've heard that said."

William Stewart eyed Jerez with undisguised disapproval. I guessed that Stewart was the sort of man who took both food and drink for granted and was not apt to become lyrical over either. There was, certainly, a practical deliberation about the way he was consuming his croquettes.

"What's all this about Marian?" he demanded, turning on Jerez, a knife clenched in one hand and a fork in the other. "How badly off is she, anyhow?"

Jerez put down his glass and gestured with wide-open hands. It was as though, with this man, he was deliberately trying to accentuate the Latin qualities in his nature. "I do not know," he said. "The dragon will not allow me to see her. Not even last night was I allowed to be with her."

It was impossible to tell whether he was genuinely worried or not. I glanced at David, thinking that he might volunteer some information, but he was picking at his food, his lips pressed tight together.

"Senhora told me this morning that Miss Russell— that she was all right," I volunteered. "There's no concussion. It wasn't even necessary to call a doctor, although I understand Senhora sat up all night with her."

"Touching," Jerez muttered under his breath. "One must toast such touching dedication."

He gestured to MacGregor, who stood waiting by the sideboard. For a long moment the old man stared back at him with what seemed to be rheumy defiance. Then, carrying a wine bottle, he shuffled toward the end of the table.

I became aware that William Stewart was delivering himself authoritatively on the subject of women drivers. "They can manage the straight-ahead sort of driving you find on dual carriageways quite adequately, of course," he boomed. "Even a child could do that. But when it comes to driving that requires snap decisions, the exercise of judgment——"

"It was my fault that Marian was injured," I said. "The brakes had given way. You must admit there was nothing either of us could have done about that. I made the decision to stop the car any way we could and put on the emergency brake."

The sharpness of my own voice startled me. There was a knot of tension inside me that my dislike of the thick-faced man across from me could not altogether justify. I was uncomfortably aware that Claire Stewart had stopped chattering, and that both she and the man who looked like Philip were listening to me.

"Don't pay any attention to William," Claire told me. For the first time I looked at her directly. She was incredibly beautiful, with porcelainlike skin and absolutely regular features. Her eyes struck the only discordant note. Oddly slanted, they were thickly fringed with dark-brown lashes that contrasted strongly with the near-white blondness of her long hair, but it was more than coloring. There was a shrewdness about those eyes which everything else about her belied. The way in which she wore her hair, the breathlessness of her voice, even the demure quality of the scoop-necked peasant blouse she was wearing, seemed deliberately to promote a childlike quality. But there was nothing childlike about those eyes. She giggled as she patted her husband's arm.

"William is absolutely dedicated to the belief that

women are basically incompetent," she went on. "Aren't you, darling?" She turned back to me. "It feeds his male ego," she said, "but you're not to take him seriously, Miss Haverlock. It's our only defense, you know: not to take men like my husband seriously."

"Don't talk nonsense, Claire," William Stewart said blandly, pushing his empty plate away from him and settling back in his chair, his hands clasped over his ample stomach.

"Darling," his wife said, "you know you like to hear me talk nonsense. You'd be appalled if I tried to be serious."

It was a light-enough exchange, but somehow it made me uncomfortable. A momentary silence fell over the table as the maids began to remove the plates. Even Jerez was silent, fingering the stem of his wineglass, apparently lost in thought.

"I was just telling Martin," Claire went on lightly, "that he must see the famous collection while he's here." Her fingers fluttered down her husband's arm. "If you've no objection, darling, I thought I might show it to him this afternoon."

So his name was Martin. Involuntarily I glanced at him, hating the fact that the simple combination of reddish hair and broad features should make my heart pound so. We were all types. There must be hundreds of men who would remind me of Philip. I was a fool to let it disconcert me.

"You won't be much use to Martin as a guide," William Stewart muttered. "You don't know the first thing about the stuff my stepmother has stashed away in that wing. Besides, it's an abominable way to spend an afternoon. I'm only quoting you. When I tried to show it to you, you lasted only through one room—not that I blame you."

"On the contrary," the man at the end of the table said. "I'd be interested."

I had not been able to tear my eyes away from his

face, and now he looked at me directly. "Perhaps," he said, "Miss Haverlock, as an expert——"

"Of course!" Jerez exclaimed, suddenly coming to life. "That's an excellent idea. From what I heard you say last night at dinner, Mr. Kubler, you already know something about Iberian art, and as you say, Irene here is an expert."

"She won't have time to give guided tours!" Claire snapped. "Isn't that right, Miss Haverlock?"

I knew that I should make some response, but instead I pretended to center my interest on the elaborate sweet that one of the maids was placing before me. Claire Stewart was right. I did not have time. More than that, I did not want to walk alone through those dimly lit rooms with a stranger who conjured up so many painful memories. But in order to respond I would have to assume a role. There was only one choice, of course: that of the crisp, no-nonsense professional woman. I knew that was what Claire expected of me, and yet for some odd reason I did not want to satisfy her. I had no intention of playing the foil to her girlishness. There was no particular difference in our ages. She and I and David were all in our mid-twenties, yet I was certain that if I gave her a chance, she would take delight in displaying me as an up-tight spinster.

I raised my eyes to Martin Kubler and smiled. "Perhaps," I said in a low voice, "if you can give me a little more time to become acquainted with the collection myself. . . ."

I quite deliberately did not finish the sentence. What I had said neither committed me nor freed me of involvement. Martin Kubler nodded, his eyes never leaving mine. Without looking at Claire Stewart, I sensed her anger. Beside me David remained silent. I heard Jerez laugh with a strange note of triumph.

"Fair enough," he said, "but perhaps Irene ought to know that she'll be doing a public service. As a psychiatrist, Mr. Kubler needs to know as much as he can about Lady Stewart before he pronounces her insane."

"Is it true that Jerez insulted Kubler?" Marian Russell asked me.

I shook my head wearily. I had spent the afternoon in the long gallery, and I was tired. It seemed the easiest part of the collection with which to start, since it contained only paintings, and most of those were large portraits. But the lighting was so poor that even with the help of the flashlight with which I had equipped myself, I had found identification difficult. At six, hot and grimy with dust, I had hurried back through the main part of the house, praying that I would not meet anyone. I had thought that I was home safe until I closed my bedroom door behind me and found Marian sitting in the chair by the window, looking as chic as when I had met her yesterday, except for the bandage that cut across the right side of her forehead.

"He implied that Kubler was deliberately going to find Lady Stewart insane," I said. "I suppose that if I had been intent on reading something into what he said, it would have been that Martin Kubler is unscrupulous."

"He is, of course," Marian said quickly. "William claims that he has an international reputation as a psychiatrist, but I've never heard of him. Bringing him here was William's idea, of course. He's determined to break that will. If anyone is unscrupulous, it's William. Still, Jerez shouldn't have said what he did, poor darling. He lets himself get carried away. Especially when he's here—he hates it so."

I stood just inside the door, looking at her. My bedroom faced the east, and the fading afternoon sun was kinder to her than the blazing sun of yesterday. Even so, her face seemed to be skinned with crumpled parchment. The deftly applied makeup accomplished nothing. One could be distracted only by her dress, a tailored white-silk sheath with a high shirtlike collar that plunged to a deep V, disclosing the lightly tanned flesh between her breasts. There, at least, the skin was smooth. I wondered what had drawn Jerez to her. When he had spoken of her in the courtyard, there had been a certain impersonal quality to his voice. But when she talked of him, it was tenderly, with an overlay of ruefulness that a woman might express in speaking of a careless child.

"Jerez told me all about it this afternoon," she went on, bracelets jangling as she reached up to touch the bandage, "directly after lunch. I believed his version of the affair, of course, but I wanted to hear it from someone else as well. For a sensitive man, Jerez is sometimes quite oblivious to the effects of what he says. And, of course, people like William irritate him so—that terrible British condescension. Jerez has his own career. Perhaps he told you. He's an interior decorator—quite well known in Lisbon. That was where we met, you see. I have an apartment there where I live part of the year, and when I wanted to redecorate last year, one of my friends recommended Jerez."

She told the story proudly, with the triumph of a woman who has quite unexpectedly attracted a personable man. For Jerez was personable. So much so that I wondered for the second time what had drawn him to this woman. I did not know her well enough to make judgments, but there was a brittle quality about her, a lack of depth. Even last night, when she had discovered that David was driving the car, she had collapsed into simple hysteria. Whatever else Jerez was, he was a complex individualist with a subtle sense of humor which I doubted whether Marian was capable of appreciating. Somehow, listening to her talk about Jerez disconcerted me, as though I sensed that at any moment she might say more than she meant to say and end by embarrassing both of us.

"I'm glad you're better," I said, deliberately changing

the subject. Going to sit on the edge of the high bed, I caught a glimpse of myself in the broad gilt-edged mirror and saw that my hair was pulled back in a tangle, that my face was dirt-stained, and that I had clearly been a fool to have worn white slacks, which in the few hours I had spent in the long gallery had turned gray. I wished that this woman would leave me alone. After a bath I knew that I might feel more human.

"It was nothing," Marian Russell said quickly. Clearly she was no more certain of how to cope with my lack of interest now than she had been yesterday. I remembered how she had washed her hands of me the day before and hoped that she would do the same thing again. This time there would be no need to sit in awkward silence in the confines of a car. All that she had to do was to get up and leave the room—my room. I waited, silent, for her to do so.

"You mustn't blame yourself for what happened," she said, crossing and uncrossing her slim legs. "Jerez told me that you defended my driving to William." A faint smile flickered across her worn face. "You kept us from going over the side of that road, you know. What we should have done—what *I* should have done—was to shift into first gear. Jerez told me that this afternoon. But I would never have thought of it—never. It was clever of you to pull the emergency brake, even if it meant I had to bang my head."

She looked at me in that same expectant manner I had been aware of yesterday. There was something curiously girl-like in these moments, as though she expected some sort of spontaneous response from me—and this in the face of my having snubbed her the day before. I gave up the idea of a bath and offered her a drink, taking the bottle of Scotch I had brought with me from the top drawer of the dresser.

"You should ring for ice, really," Marian chattered happily, "but I know why you might hesitate. I mean, one feels as though one is here on sufferance, don't you agree? At least I do. And Jerez feels the same way. The only person who's made to feel at home here is—is David."

The moment she said his name I knew that all the rest—all the concern over what Jerez had said to William Stewart, all the hesitant offerings of friendship—had been for this purpose. Yesterday she had wanted me to take sides in some kind of vaguely defined internecine struggle, and now she wanted something from me again. Only this time it involved her son. My first response was of resentment mixed with a feeling of helplessness, and she sensed this.

"Jerez told me that I shouldn't talk to you about David," she said, draining her glass and getting up to pour more. "He likes you, you know—very much. He says that you're very sensible. That's something that I'm not, I'm afraid. I act from instinct." She went into the bathroom, and the rest of what she said was lost in the sound of running water as she mixed her drink.

"And so," she said, coming back into the bedroom, "I decided that no matter what he said, I'd ask you to help me."

I sank back on the bed and lit a cigarette. "I don't know what I could possibly do to help you," I said.

I was not trying to repulse her as I had the day before. What I said was the simple truth, but she shook her head and came to stand by the bed. She looked down at me, and her face sagged into even deeper lines. Despite the eyeliner and the mascara, her eyes had that strangely exposed look of one who usually wears glasses. Yesterday there had been a veneer of hardness about her that had made it easier for me to explain that I did not want to involve myself in her affairs. Today she seemed to be doing everything that she could do to put herself in as vulnerable a position as possible.

"Jerez overheard part of what David said to you during

lunch," she said slowly, "about whether or not he should stay at Alcombra as long as I'm here. Jerez told me that David said that he didn't want to hurt me."

"That's true," I said.

She turned away from me restlessly and paced to the window. A peacock was seated on the ledge, pressed against the glass. As she approached, the bird turned and stared curiously at her with beady eyes. Marian did not appear to notice him.

"You don't know what it meant to me to hear that," she said, bowing her head. There was, I thought, something schizophrenic about her appearance. Standing with her back to me, so slim, her hair so beautifully coiffured, she might have been a young woman. Then she turned, and the illusion was broken.

"You must have been curious last night," she said, almost defiantly. "The fact that he didn't recognize me——"

"It doesn't matter," I said.

"But it does to me! This is the only time I've been in the same house with him since three weeks after he was born. I mean, it's a chance, the only chance I may have, to make him understand why I—why I gave him up, let my aunt take the responsibility for him. I know from what she's told me that she taught him to hate me. Now I have to explain it all to him. You don't know what it's been like all these years, knowing that I made a mistake."

"Go to him now, then," I said in a low voice. "Talk to him."

She raised her glass to her lips, and I saw that her hands were shaking. "That's what Jerez said," she whispered. "With him everything is so simple. He doesn't understand that I can't. I can't! But David will talk to you. You're the same age. He likes you. He wouldn't have said the things he said to you during luncheon if he didn't trust you."

"He and I are strangers," I protested. "He was only explaining to me why he couldn't stay here."

"He wouldn't have tried to explain if there wasn't some —some rapport," she insisted. "If you won't help me, he may leave, or I will have to go myself—one or the other. If her ladyship has anything to do with it, it will be me."

"Perhaps," I said, "it would be better if you left Alcombra."

For a moment her eyes narrowed. It was the first time I had seen guile in her face. "You don't know what my position is," she said slowly. "If my aunt insists on this— this insane idea of turning Alcombra into a museum, it's going to mean that every cent of the estate, except for what she leaves Senhora and MacGregor, will be involved. I've got to try to salvage something for myself. It's only fair that I should. My mother was her sister, after all. When Mother was still alive, she always promised her that there would be something. . . . But then she became obsessed with this collection. It's gone on for fifty years. When I was a child, we were poor. I mean, really poor. Probably you don't understand what it means to go without everything that makes life civilized. I could have had a proper education if her ladyship could have spared one moment's thought from all this." She wildly waved the hand in which she was holding the glass, and what was left of the drink was spilled onto the carpet. She did not appear to notice.

"My mother swallowed her pride and came here begging. My father was dead. We needed help, and she promised. And in the end there were a few hundred pounds. We could have managed better if we hadn't always had to remember that she was sitting on a fortune. If she had been what she should have been to us, there never would have been a David."

She broke off. Sinking down on a chair, she buried her face in her hands. "His father was no one I could have married," she said in a muffled voice. "The kind of man I never would have met if we hadn't had to live the life we did: cheap pensions, always on the move trying to find some place less expensive, the odd jobs. I didn't even have the training to be a secretary. It killed my mother in the end. It wasn't my having David. *She* always said that it was, but that's simply not true."

The way in which she spat out the word "she" told me that the reference was to Lady Stewart. Marian was making herself quite clear—too clear. I did not want her to go on, and yet I did not know how to stanch the flow of words.

"I couldn't keep him—not with things the way they were. My mother wrote to her, and she offered to take him. I thought at the time that it was—it was the first really kind thing that she had done, until I realized that as far as she was concerned, I was never to see him again. Not even when I married Arthur Russell. That was the only reason I married him. I thought that then she would let me have the child back. He was a doctor—a fairly good practice in England. When he died five years ago, he left me enough to live on. But there's always been this to think about. Alcombra. And her. She always took everything she wanted, including my child."

It was a magnificent performance, and it was false as hell. I did not even attempt to say anything when she had finished. For the moment I no longer pitied her. She had had no right to make me play audience to this kind of act, and yet I knew that I might be making a wrong judgment. Obviously she had been possessed for years by her own obsessions. The point was that I had never wanted to make any sort of judgment about her at all.

Her hands collapsed from her face, but she did not turn to look at me. The room was warm with the captured sunlight of the day. Outside the window the peacock still stared in at us. I felt the same uneasiness I had felt the night before, as though we were not alone in this room.

"Will you talk to David?"

I realized that I would be willing to do anything to make her leave me alone.

"Yes," I said wearily. "What do you want me to tell him?"

"I don't know." She spoke almost impatiently. "Tell him what kind of person I am."

"I don't know what kind of person you are."

"You know enough about me. Just let him know the kind of pressures I'm under. He's only known her side of the story. I don't know what he thinks of me. Don't you see? I tried to explain this to Jerez. I can't talk to David until I know what he thinks about me, how he'll react. I couldn't stand it if he simply shut me off. I have to be certain that he'll listen."

"All right," I said. "I'll talk to him tonight if you like."

She rose and started toward the door, with her face still averted from me.

"He can't leave," she said, "not now. Make him promise he won't leave until I've talked to him."

"I'll try," I said.

She did not thank me, and for the moment I did not care. As soon as the door closed behind her, I leaned back against the pillows and fell into a dreamless sleep.

When I awoke, the room was dark. Outside the window a thin streak of moonlight touched the pines. The air was stuffy with the smell of cigarette smoke, and my head was thick with unremembered dreams. When the tapping came, I remembered that that was the sound that had awakened me. Stumbling off the high canopied bed, I switched on a light and went to the door, but there was no one in the long, dimly lit corridor. Somewhere in the distance a woman laughed, and then there was silence.

The door closed behind me, and I heard the sound again and realized that something was striking one of the windows. My first thought was that a peacock might be pecking at the glass. Still groggy with sleep, I went first to one window and then to another, throwing them open to the coolness of the night. As I opened the last, something struck me lightly on the arm, and I saw a pebble fall to the carpet at my feet.

"Irene."

It was a man's voice. Leaning out into the darkness, I saw someone standing below, a shadow faintly touched by moonlight.

"It's me. David. Are you all right?"

Instantly I was wide awake.

"You woke me," I whispered.

"Sorry. I was worried when you didn't turn up for dinner."

Dinner. It was later than I thought, then. I was suddenly uncomfortably aware of hunger.

"Come outside," David hissed. "It's a beautiful night. I've managed to round up some food. We'll have a picnic on the hill."

I laughed. The idea was suddenly irresistible. As though to urge me on, the moon broke through a thin veil of clouds, splashing the courtyard with white light.

"Wait for me where you are," I said, not bothering to mute my voice. "I won't be long."

It was strange to feel like a schoolgirl again—strange and exhilarating. Throwing off my crumpled slacks and shirt, I showered quickly, forgetting in my rush to cover my hair. Standing naked in front of the long bathroom mirror, I combed the long, damp strands straight down about my face in dark sheets. There was nothing of the competent professional woman in the image that stared back at me. My eyes were still heavy with sleep, and my cheeks were flushed. I knew that I looked more like eighteen than twenty-five, and I was glad.

Quickly I slipped on a pair of brief lavender-jersey shorts and a matching long-sleeve top. A long wrap-around flowered skirt, which opened in the front to my waist, and sandals completed the outfit. During the past few years I had bought most of my clothes to please

Philip, traditional classic dresses and suits, but this outfit had been chosen as a deliberate act of defiance the day after we had broken off our engagement. I had told myself as I stood in the shop on Oxford Street, watching the girl wrap the package, that the moment marked my emancipation from him. But that had not been true, of course. No one can purchase for twelve pounds one's freedom from another human being, but as I hurried out into the passageway, the full skirt billowing about my bare legs, I thought that perhaps there was just a chance my release would come sooner than I had dared to hope.

I turned to the left. When I had come back that afternoon from the wing where the collection was housed, I had come across the courtyard and discovered a side door that led to a deserted hallway from which narrow stairs ran up to the second floor. The route suited me much better than the front approach, which meant crossing the vast hallway under the penetrating glare of the cherubs who flitted across the painted ceiling. Using the front door increased the chance that I might meet someone, even if only the dour MacGregor, and tonight I particularly did not want to meet anyone. When he had thrown those pebbles against my window, David had set a mood—a mood I did not want broken.

It was only when I reached the bend in the hallway that I realized that one of those closed doors I had hurried past this afternoon was the door to Lady Stewart's bedroom. I had been so new to the house when Senhora had first taken me with her that directions had eluded me, but now I heard the booming resonance of a voice that could be no one but her ladyship's, raised in anger. At the same moment a door ahead of me opened to disgorge her stepson, with Senhora close on his heels. Without rationalizing what I was doing, I drew back behind one of the innumerable pieces of statuary which lined the hall and held myself motionless, expecting them to pass me. Instead, they drew together only a few feet away from the door and began to talk in low voices. At first I did not even try to listen. My own impatience to get outside seemed to stop my ears. Then I heard Senhora spit out the name of Martin Kubler.

"You should have known better than to have brought him here," she said. I could not see her, but I could imagine all too well the glittering eyes, the taut, dark face.

William Stewart answered her, but the words blurred together until they lost themselves in undertones.

"She'll never agree to seeing him now that she knows what he is," the woman hissed.

"That's not my fault," the man replied, no longer making an attempt to whisper. "I brought Martin here as my guest—nothing more. How Caravels found out that he's a psychiatrist I don't know. Marian always did associate with fools. He put a screw in things, blurting it out that way at the table—the idiot. It's to his advantage as much as it is to ours to have her declared incompetent. I suppose it was MacGregor who told her."

"Keep your voice down," Senhora told him. "Of course it was MacGregor. He reports everything. He always has. Why do you expect she keeps him on? Not that it matters now who told her. You might as well send Kubler back to wherever he came from."

"You said you'd help. . . ."

The voices were nearer now, and I knew that the two must be moving toward where I stood. I pressed myself closer against the wall, realizing that I had been a fool to have hidden myself like this in the first place. I should have walked past them and kept on going. It would be humiliating to have them find me like this—and David was waiting.

"I promised nothing," the woman was saying. "As far as I'm concerned, she's no different than she has been for the past thirty years. I told you before that if you brought this to court, I'd swear that she's as sane as I am."

They were beside the statue now. I could see Senhora's sweatered arm. In another moment. . . .

I must have been involuntarily pressing to the left, because suddenly the statue gave way, rocking on its base. Reaching out to steady it, I found myself looking straight into Senhora's scowling face.

"So," she said triumphantly, "you were eavesdropping, Miss Haverlock."

I opened my mouth to protest and realized suddenly that there was no explanation I could reasonably make. They would not understand if I told them that I had wanted to leave the house without seeing anyone. Why should they? Yet I could not bear the thought that they should be left to believe that I was interested enough in their affairs to want to overhear anything they might say. Trapped, I answered one question with another.

"Why should I want to eavesdrop on you?" I said carefully. "Actually I was on my way out of the house."

"By way of the side door?" Senhora's eyes were narrow slits of suspicion.

"Front way, back way, what does it matter?" William Stewart said gruffly, and I realized that he was as disconcerted as I, as anxious as I to end this encounter. He plunged his hands nervously in and out of the pockets of his blue blazer, which was buttoned tightly over his stomach.

"If you intended to try to see Lady Stewart tonight, you must understand that it's out of the question," Senhora said sharply. "She's not at all well. There are far too many people in this house making demands on her. From now on, any instructions that she has for you will be conveyed through me."

"That's perfectly agreeable to me," I said, trying to pass her.

"It's not at all certain," the woman said, moving to the left so that she blocked my path, "that Lady Stewart will wish the inventory to be completed after all."

"I'm afraid," I said stiffly, "that if it comes to that, she will have to instruct me personally to leave. There are certain instructions that I would be willing to have 'conveyed,' as you put it, through you, and others that I would not. In fact, I think that her solicitors in London would be very much concerned if I were dismissed without a personal interview with her."

"Are you threatening me?" Senhora's voice slashed its way through the silence that followed my remark.

I had not intended to be drawn into any sort of altercation with this woman, but I found myself possessed, quite suddenly, with an absorbing fury.

"I'm explaining to you what will and will not be acceptable to me," I said. "If there is any question about the inventory being completed, I will have to know now. My time is valuable. I don't intend to put in weeks of work here for nothing."

William Stewart cleared his throat nervously. "I think," he said, "that we ought to talk this out in private."

"There's nothing to 'talk out,' " I told him. "Under the circumstances I'm going to have to insist on seeing Lady Stewart in the morning."

"She's much too ill," Senhora began.

"I'll take her doctor's word for that," I said. "She *is* being attended by a doctor, I take it. If she's had a serious relapse since I saw her this morning, he should have seen her today. *Did* he see her?"

The hall was very dimly lighted, but I could see that Senhora's face was flushed with anger.

"I think that we must trust Senhora in this affair," William Stewart said hurriedly.

"You may prefer to trust her, but I see no reason why I should," I snapped. "I intend to get in touch with her doctor tomorrow, and unless there is any reason why I should not see her, I intend to get this matter of the inventory settled once and for all then."

Senhora reached out and gripped my arm, her nails digging through the jersey into my flesh. "Marian Russell put you up to this, didn't she?" she asked, and then, turning to the man beside her: "I told you. . . ."

I did not want to hear any more. It took all my self-control not to push her away from me. My hand settled on hers, disengaging her fingers, and then I was running down the passageway and down the narrow stairs and out through the narrow door into the caressing warmth of the moonlit night.

I did not see David until he caught me by the shoulders and turned me to face him. His face was a white streak in the darkness.

"Where the devil have you been? It's been at least fifteen minutes since you switched off the light in your bedroom."

I shook my head. The night air settled like a gentle touch about me, and although David's voice was impatient, his hands were gentle, too.

"I don't want to talk about it now," I said. "I met someone when I was coming out of the house. That's all."

Instantly he was alert. He moved away from me, and I could hear a thin edge of hostility in his voice. "My mother?" he said.

"No. Only Senhora—and William Stewart."

David whispered an exclamation. "What were those two doing together?" he demanded. "They hate one another's guts."

"It was something about Kubler," I said. "They were coming out of your great-aunt's bedroom."

He whistled softly. "Why in God's name——"

"I don't want to talk about it now," I repeated, keeping my voice light, trying to recapture the mood in which I had left my room minutes before. "Besides, I'm hungry. Remember, I didn't have any dinner."

"I remember." He laughed and took my hand, bending at the same time to pick up what appeared to be a wicker basket. "All right. Let's go."

Weaving our way along the gravel paths, we passed the stone pig and emerged from the courtyard at the back of the wing where the collection was kept. Soon we were climbing up a narrow track between the pine trees. It was too dark for me to see where we were going, but David seemed to know the way. I was out of breath by the time we reached the top of the rise and emerged into the full glow of the moonlight. Below us the house stretched itself like a massive shadowy hand, dotted with a few lights.

"Here," David said. "Just over the top a bit. There's a hollow. I used to come here when I was a boy. I don't expect we can see the river."

But we could see it. Far below us in the distance it sparkled like a thin trail of white silk. On either side of it the land seemed to rise in terraced steps.

"The vineyards," David said. "My God, it's beautiful. I'd almost forgotten."

We sat down on the rough grass, and he groped in the basket for a white cloth, which he spread carefully in front of us. "There's cold chicken," he said, "and cheese, rolls and butter, and wine. I took the decanter from the alcove outside the dining room. It was all I could lay my hands on. MacGregor guards the wine cellar like a gorgon."

I ate as though I were famished, and he watched me in silence. We drank the thick, rich port from wineglasses he had brought wrapped in napkins. A slight breeze rose, brushing my still damp hair. Perhaps it was the wine or the food or the moon-glossed view, but I felt incredibly happy.

"Well," David said, throwing himself supine beside me, "what do you think of the menagerie now that you've seen it? God knows, if I'd known they were all here, I would have turned around and let you and my mother make your own way down the side of that mountain."

"Even if you'd known that your great-aunt was dying?"

He laughed. "You don't mince words, do you? No, if you want the truth, I still wouldn't have come—to appropriate one of her terms, not if it meant joining the vultures."

He raised his hands, cupping them to his lips, and a shrill whistling sound pierced the night. I realized that he was blowing on a piece of grass, and suddenly I remembered long summer afternoons at the house my father had rented once in Kent and lying flat on my back for hours, watching the clouds change their shapes. I had amused myself then, as David was now, by blowing on strips of grass—and watching ants crawl over my fingers. For a moment I ached with the awareness that for so long there had been nothing in my life to remind me of those long sunlit hours.

"No," David said abruptly, rolling on his side toward me. "No, I take back what I just said. I would have come anyway if I thought that she needed me, and I think, you know, that she does. Oh, she can keep up the old facade when she's not in too much pain. She always did like to play the tyrant. But she's losing her grip on Alcombra, and she knows it. And that's why I'm going to stay. If she wants this place turned into a museum, that's the way it's going to be."

"Do you think the others could stop it from happening? I know what her stepson is trying to do, but——"

"You mean his bringing Kubler here? That may have already backfired on dear old William, you know."

"Because Lady Stewart knows that Kubler is a psychiatrist?"

David shifted onto his back again, spreading his arms wide over his head. "No, although that will present problems if she finds out."

"She already knows," I told him. "MacGregor apparently told her what Jerez said at luncheon."

David chuckled. "What about Jerez?" he said. "I haven't seen much of him, but he seems like a genuine character —too much of a character to have latched onto my mother."

"You can't really say that," I murmured. "You don't know her, do you?"

"No! No, I don't know her!" He threw himself into a sitting position, pressing his face against his knees. "But I'm talking about Kubler. I had a chance to talk to him this afternoon—not about why he's here, not directly. But I got the impression that William didn't give him the whole story. I take it that he thought he was here at Lelia's request. Now that he knows that isn't so, I think he'll leave. He's not a bad sort—no charlatan, at any rate. It's like William not to let his right hand know what his left hand is doing. That's why he's in financial trouble."

"What do you mean?"

"Oh, he hasn't talked about it to me. We aren't what you'd call friends. He was in his early thirties when I first remember him. He lived here at Alcombra until I was ten and his father died. Presumably he helped manage the vineyards, but I don't think that he actually did anything much. He certainly wasn't a happy man. Young as I was, I realized that. He and Lelia never did get along. She likes people who perform—who do something."

David took up the decanter and poured us both another glass of port. The moonlight flickered on the glasses.

"Anyway, when his father died, he was furious because he'd been left only enough to set himself up in business. In the end Lelia told him to get out. He went to England and bought into an export-import firm that deals in Portuguese wines. Now and then he'd turn up here begging for a handout in a refined kind of way. When I was sent away to school, I lost track of him. We never happened to visit Alcombra at the same time. This is the first I've seen of him for nearly ten years, and I can't say that I think age has particularly improved him."

"How do you know that he needs money?"

David laughed. "That's thanks to Claire," he said. "I don't know where William found her, but I'm willing to bet that he handed her a story about being heir to Lelia's fortune. She doesn't strike me as the sort of girl who'd have attached herself to someone like him without pretty substantial motivation." He rolled over to face me again.

"More wine?" he said.

I shook my head.

"Listen, Irene," he said in a low voice. "Do you really want me to talk about this? From what Jerez said tonight, I take it that you'd rather not be too involved in the family's little crises."

"Jerez!" I smiled and let myself slide down until I was lying, looking up at both David and the moon. "He's incredible. What did he say about me?"

"He gave us all a little lecture over the soup, as a matter of fact," David told me. "I think he got it into his head that you hadn't come down to dinner because you felt that we were, somehow, bearing in on you. He said that he had made a mistake himself in suggesting that you show Kubler around the collection. In fact, he went on at considerable length about how you should be let alone to do what you came here to do."

I turned my cheek against the grass and smelled the warm thick scent of summer. The moonlight was so bright that I could see the small white flowers nestled close to the ground. I was not certain whether I wanted David to go on talking about the family or not, but so far it was the only link between us. And besides, I had promised Marian. . . . I swept the thought of her to the back of my mind. I owed her nothing, and I did not want to risk anything that would destroy this moment.

"Tell me about Claire," I said. "I'm a woman, and you know about women and curiosity."

"Yes, you're a woman," David said slowly. I closed my eyes against the moonlight as he bent closer over me, and I felt his lips brush my face. For a moment neither of us spoke, and then with a sudden sharpness, he repeated Claire's name.

"She had a lot to say to me over dinner," he said. "I think she's more interested in enticing Kubler, actually. But he wasn't interested. I don't think he had a word for anyone—probably wondering how he was going to extricate himself from all this."

I opened my eyes and saw that he was sitting up again, staring off across the valley.

"Claire?" I said gently.

"When you get to know me better," David said, "you'll find that I have a very annoying habit. I rarely speak directly to the point. It takes a long time for me to tell a story properly, and tonight for some reason I think that it's going to take longer than usual."

He turned and looked down at me, grinning. "Claire," he said, "apparently decided that I was the only halfway-acceptable substitute for Kubler and monopolized me during the meal—not that she had to compete with anyone else to do that, you understand. William never did care for me, and I think Jerez hasn't quite made me out. And then, of course, there was my mother. Under the circumstances there wasn't much chance that the two of us would launch into a stimulating conversation about old times. In fact, she scarcely looked at me."

"Claire," I said.

"Yes, Claire. Well, as I said, she talked nonstop—not about herself, you understand. She's far too clever for that. But about London and the latest shows. I take it she wishes she were back there, and it's only a guess, but I think she was trying to make it appear that when she is there, she and William circulate in a far more glamorous circle than I think is probable."

He shrugged his shoulders. "Another thing I ought to warn you about," he said, "is that I'm inclined to be a little intolerant of people I don't like, and I don't like Claire. I think she guessed as much, but she kept up the game. Asked me about my work at university. Actually pretended an overwhelming interest in Georgian poetry. God!"

Pushing himself to his feet, he revolved in a circle, arms outstretched, and flung himself back on the ground, face down in a pool of moonlight, laughing. "What are we doing talking about someone like Claire Stewart? Let's discuss the relationship between a full moon and madness."

"Don't be a fool," I teased him, sitting up and wrapping my skirt around my bare legs. The clouds had appeared again, and as I spoke, one swept across the moon. The river below disappeared, and so did he. The breeze was stronger now, and I felt suddenly chilled. "Come on, now," I said. "What did Claire say that makes you think that her husband is desperate for money?"

"I didn't say he was desperate." David's voice seemed far away. "I said he needed it. Claire told me that the bottom had fallen out of the business he invested in. She just slipped that detail into the conversation in the process of telling me she had been trying to convince William that she should go back to modeling—high-fashion modeling. She made a great point of that. Irene. . . ."

In the darkness I could not even see the outline of him, but suddenly his hand was cupping my face. If the moon had not been behind a cloud, it would have been all right. If I could have seen him, I would not have conjured up Philip's face. I leaned to the side and drew my face away.

"Sorry," I heard David say. "Sorry! Sorry! Sorry!"

The moon sped into view, windblown now, in flight. Before it disappeared, I saw that David had risen to his feet and that he was holding the decanter to his lips, draining the last of the wine. I suppose I was confused. Otherwise I would never have mentioned Marian at that precise moment. But I had to say something—anything.

"Your mother came to talk to me today," I said.

"Did she?" His voice was cold.

"She wanted me to speak to you. I——"

"Is that why you came out here with me tonight? Carrying messages?"

"No," I protested. "No. I came because I wanted to. It doesn't matter about her now. I'm sorry."

"But it does matter," he said. For a moment his face was illuminated in a glare of white light, and then the darkness engulfed him again. "What did she want you to say to me?"

"She wants to talk to you herself, but——"

"Then why doesn't she?"

Suddenly I wanted to weep. What was it Philip had said to me once? That in the end I spoiled every moment. That had hurt, but I had been so certain that it was just because he was he and I. . . .

"She wants to explain," I said in a low voice.

"I imagine that she does. It's a good time for it now, isn't it? Now that I'm no longer a responsibility. Now that there's just a chance that I may inherit some of that money she's had her eye on for so long."

"But you aren't going to inherit anything. Senhora and MacGregor will have something, but all the rest will go to maintaining the museum." The words burst out of me involuntarily.

"And how do you know that?" He might have been a stranger. Whatever our relationship had been, it had floundered when I had drawn away from him.

"I can't remember," I said. "Someone said. It doesn't matter."

"That's one of your favorite phrases, isn't it? 'It doesn't matter.' But everything does matter, you know—to someone."

The bitterness had gone from his voice now, leaving it flat and expressionless.

"She simply wanted me to tell you that she—she doesn't dare approach you. She thinks that Lady Stewart has turned you against her. She doesn't want to be rebuffed."

For a moment he did not speak. "I suppose," he said, "none of us want to be rebuffed, but sometimes you have to take the chance. Come. We'll go back now."

He did not speak again as we made our way back down the hill. He took my hand but only to help me find the way. And the moon stayed behind the clouds.

CHAPTER

4

It must have been past midnight when I reached my bed-room to find MacGregor waiting for me outside the door. The house had seemed totally silent. Sleeping. The front door locked. David had opened it with a large key that fitted noiselessly in the old-fashioned keyhole, and we had parted at the top of the stairs, leaving the silence in the vast hall below us unbroken.

I was so lost in my own sense of depression that I did not notice the old man until my hand was on the knob of my bedroom door. Only a single table lamp glowed at the far end of the long corridor, and when he moved out of the shadows that had hidden him, I cried out, startled. His creased face was set in its usual grim lines of disapproval.

"Her ladyship wants to see you," he said in a low voice thick with a Scottish burr. "Come with me."

I wanted to protest. I wanted to tell him that I would

see her in the morning. But then I remembered what
Senhora had said to me about the fact that from now
on she would act as a messenger for her mistress, and that
there was some doubt about whether or not Lady Stewart
would want the inventory to be completed. I had taken a
bold line with her in my anger, insisting on my right to see
the woman who had employed me. I had made threats that
involved contacting an unknown doctor. It seemed as
though all that had happened years ago, and now—now I
was not at all certain that I wanted to stay at Alcombra.
Perhaps it would be best to put the matter straight now,
no matter what the time.

And so I followed the old man to her room. The thick
carpet muffled our footsteps. Only when I saw the light
shining around the rim of her door did I realize that I was
tense with nervousness. If Senhora was with her, there
would be difficulties. And I did not want any more
difficulties.

But there was no one in the long high-ceilinged room
except the old woman, propped up in the canopied bed
as I had seen her that morning. She nodded past me at
MacGregor as I came toward her, and he went outside,
closing the door noiselessly behind him.

"He will see that we are not interrupted," Lady Stewart
said when I reached the bed. The single light that burned
on the table beside her made a white mask of her face.
"Sit down. Yes, there. Move the chair up a bit. Senhora
has ears like a hawk."

"She told me earlier this evening that you weren't well,"
I said. The chair was so close to the bed that I was caught
in the pool of light. Beyond us the room receded into
darkness. The air was heavy with the smell of medicine,
harsh acrid odors.

"It escapes me why a dying woman should be expected
to be well, as you put it," Lady Stewart said dryly.
"Hand me that handkerchief, will you, my dear? There,
on the table."

There was something different about her tonight, I realized. This morning she had been tense, defiant, determined to demonstrate that she was a powerful woman. Perhaps it had been the presence of Senhora in the room which had made her so harsh. Even physically she seemed to have changed. I remembered the way her gnarled hand had gripped the shawl about her heavy shoulders, the way she had kept pushing herself up from the pillows, the sudden viciousness with which she had struck out with her cane. Now she seemed to exude only an overpowering weariness, which softened the thick, hawk-nosed face. There was nothing in those dark eyes except a certain curiosity as she looked at me. I guessed that this morning she had been too intent on creating an impression to consider me as a person. I waited, but she did not speak.

Uncomfortably I glanced down at my crossed legs and saw that the slit skirt had fallen away from them and that my skin was flecked with bits of dry grass.

"I've been outside," I said with sudden awkwardness.

"I thought you might have been." Her lips curled in a sly smile. "Do you think it's wise to walk about alone at this time of night?"

"I wasn't alone," I said.

She waited.

"I was with David."

"Ah, yes." The smile faded. "And what do you think of my grandnephew?"

"He's. . . ." I realized suddenly that I did not know what to say. Somehow I did not want to make the usual pat comments.

"I think a good deal of him," Lady Stewart said. "Tell me, Miss Haverlock, do you think it's wise of him to stay here?"

"If he wants to stay. . . ."

For the first time since I had come into the room she moved restlessly against the pillows.

"I told him that he needn't feel obliged to see me

dead," she said with sudden harshness, "but I didn't ask you to come here to listen to me ramble on about matters that can't possibly concern you. Tell me. Have you looked at the collection?"

"Yes," I said, relieved. "I spent the afternoon in the long gallery."

"Ah!" Patches of color came into the white cheeks. "You saw the portrait of me, then."

"It's a magnificent thing," I said truthfully.

"I'd like to see it again before I die," the old woman said slowly. "I expect you'll think I'm a fool, but every day of my life that I've been in this house, I've gone to look at it. I haven't looked in mirrors for years if I could help it, but that portrait. . . . I was just twenty-five when it was painted, and as I got older—one doesn't change that much inside, you know. When I looked at that portrait, I could forget what the years were doing to me. Time is cruel, my dear. You don't know that yet, but you will."

She paused, and for a moment her broad face was convulsed with an expression of pain.

"No," she said as I started to rise. "It's all right." And then, pressing the handkerchief to her mouth: "I hate this, you know. It should have happened suddenly. I always hoped that it would happen suddenly. Now everything's failing me. It's hard to remember. . . . What were we talking about?" Her voice rose desperately. "You see, I can't remember what we were talking about."

"The long gallery," I said in a low voice, "the Sargent portrait. You'd asked me——"

"If you'd started with the inventory. Yes, that was what I wanted to know." Her eyes softened with relief. "Can it be done in the time I set? Can you do it in three weeks?"

"I think so, yes," I said, "if you still want it done."

She seemed to stiffen against the pillows. "Why would you ask that?" she demanded. "Of course I want it done."

I decided to be frank. "I talked with Senhora tonight,"

I said. "She implied that you might change your mind."

"Don't listen to her!" The old woman tried to push herself away from the pillows. "Do you understand that, Miss Haverlock? Don't listen to her."

She let herself grow limp again, breathing heavily. I knew that I was taking a risk to go on. I was not even certain of the nature of this woman's illness. I did not want to bring on any sort of attack, and yet. . . .

"She told me that I would not be seeing you again," I said slowly, "that any directions you might want to give me would come through her."

"I thought I knew what I could expect from her," the old woman muttered, her voice so low that I had to lean forward to hear her, "but she's like the others."

"She may simply feel that it would tire you to talk to me," I said soothingly.

She shook her head back and forth against the pillow. "Would you have believed her," she said, "if I hadn't sent MacGregor for you? I suspected that something was wrong, you see. The doctor should have come today. I don't know what's going on any more. I. . . ." Her voice trailed off into silence.

"No," I said. "I wasn't willing to accept what she said. I told her that I was going to insist on seeing you in the morning, that it would be necessary for your doctor to tell me himself that you were too ill to see me."

The old woman's eyes caught and held mine, and suddenly I could see the remnants of the beauty Sargent had captured. "I like you, Miss Haverlock," she said. "No, it's more than that. I trust you, and besides David, there's no one else in this house I can trust. I suppose I can't be certain even about the doctor." She paused. "Do you know about the man William brought here?"

I nodded.

"He's not going to see me," she said, her voice cracking on the words. "I'm not mad."

"No," I said slowly, "you're not mad."

Her clawlike hand crawled across the coverlet toward mine. Her fingers were cold despite the oppressive warmth of the room.

"They may say," she whispered, "that I imagined—oh, a good many things. And it's odd, you know. I haven't admitted this to anyone before, but I do have the feeling that—as though the walls were closing in."

"You could tell them all to go," I said. "You could dismiss Senhora."

She laughed then, although the sound she made was very unlike a laugh; it was deep in her throat. Then the sound turned into a racking cough, which she tried to stifle with her handkerchief.

"No, it's all right," she gasped as I half rose from my chair. And then: "What was that?" Her voice sank to a whisper. "Do you hear someone outside the door?"

I listened, aware of a sudden chill of fear. There was no sound.

"Senhora's room is next to this one," the old woman murmured. "Thank God there's no communicating door. MacGregor will give us some warning, at least, if she comes."

"But that shouldn't be necessary," I insisted. "All of this shouldn't be necessary. If you don't trust her, let her go. It shouldn't be difficult to find a nurse. You could. . . ."

The old woman closed her eyes. "No, my dear," she said. "You don't understand, and I should warn you. For your own sake, you shouldn't let anyone know that you've said what you have to me. I know these people better than you could ever know them. I know what they're capable of."

In that moment it occurred to me that I might have been wrong. Perhaps, I thought, she is mad. Her situation was difficult. I could see that. She had been a woman accustomed all her life to controlling others, but she implied a threatening situation that could not exist. In all

probability Senhora simply wanted to keep her from
becoming excited. Lady Stewart had deliberately over-
tired herself with me during that morning interview, as
she was overtiring herself now. As for Marian and William, they were probably both clinging to the hope that
something would happen that would change this woman's
plans for Alcombra. But that was natural, too.

"You're tired," I said, rising, "and everything is settled
between us. I'll complete the inventory. You can depend
on me to be as quick as I can be. And then——"

"Wait." Her eyes flickered open, and her grip on my
hand tightened. "There was something else. I've made a
list—a list of all the things in the collection that I can
remember. It's not at all complete. I wouldn't have needed
you if I could have remembered everything, but I've been
afraid. . . . It was the real reason I wanted the inventory
made. There are so many things of value. It would be so
easy for someone to take what they wanted. I have to
know. . . ."

She began to cough again. Leaning over her, I smoothed
the white hair back from her forehead.

"Don't talk any more," I said in a low voice. "I think
you're probably wrong. They wouldn't have stolen from
you, but I'll make a careful check. You only have to
give me the list, and I'll do what you want me to do."

The eighth item on the list was missing. I stood staring
at the spidery handwriting on the sheet of white-linen
stationery for many minutes before being struck by the full
significance of the simple fact that an eighteenth-century
silver snuffbox was not in the glass case where it should
have been.

The list that Lady Stewart had given me the previous
night described about a hundred of her possessions. There
was a smattering of everything: antique candelabra, bits
of furniture, small bronzes, and jewelry. Paintings, however, predominated the list. Beside each item she had

indicated where it should be found. Evidently there had
been some doubt in her mind whether she would be able
to talk to me as she had, for a letter accompanied the
list, a letter explaining why she wanted me to make this
particular check. "No one has been given permission to
move a single object," she had written. "If any one of
these things is not in its proper place, I must know at
once. If for some reason it is impossible for you to
see me personally, send a message through MacGregor."

I remembered how the old man had been standing
patiently outside Lady Stewart's door last night when I
came into the dim light of the corridor. He had not
answered when I murmured goodnight to him, and as I
went down the corridor, I had heard a door click open.
When I looked back, he had disappeared, presumably into
Lady Stewart's room. The relationship of the two old people was an intriguing one. There was something in Mac-
Gregor of the caricature of the loyal family servant, and
yet, as I had undressed, I remembered suddenly that
when she had said that she trusted me and that she
trusted David as well, she had not mentioned Mac-
Gregor's name.

I took out my notebook and began to jot down a
message, and then I paused. I had no way of knowing
how she would react when she knew that something was
missing, and it was all too possible that the snuffbox was
actually there somewhere in the five rooms. Her memory
could have failed her. With the mind's eye, it was simpli-
city itself to see an object in a place in which it had never
been. I decided to check the rest of the list as quickly as
I could. If there were a number of things missing, I would
have no choice but to let her know, but with the reminder
that the completed inventory might find them rediscovered.

It was so early in the morning that I did not feel as
though I was taking any time from what I should be
doing in the long gallery. I had hoped to complete the
inventory of the gallery today, and with that in mind, I

had set my alarm for six. The events of the night and day before had accomplished some sort of change in attitude in me, or perhaps it was simply that I felt a new assurance. I had taken a sleeping pill to get to sleep so that I would not think of David and the picnic in the moonlight. I had often taken sleeping pills when I had been engaged to Philip—and afterward, as well. It was like a welcome return to sink into a dreamless sleep. I had awakened determined to do what I had come here for as quickly as possible, and with no interference. As for the sort of restriction that Senhora and the housekeeper set on the serving of meals, I was no longer willing to put up with that nonsense. I intended to start work at seven, and I was not about to do so without having breakfast.

Dressed in brown slacks and a blouse which would not show the dirt, I had descended promptly at six-thirty to the kitchens at the back of the house. The servants were having their breakfast, seated around a long rough-wooden table in the center of a dark-beamed room equipped with a massive old-fashioned stove and an iron sink. A plump, gray-haired woman was seated at the head of the table, MacGregor at the foot. Four neatly uniformed maids lined the sides, and at a separate small table nearby sat a man whose weather-wrinkled face seemed to indicate that he was the gardener; beside him was the boy who had carried my luggage the day before. Everyone except MacGregor had stared at me in astonishment when I introduced myself and explained why I was down so early. The housekeeper had been obviously flustered and protested in Portuguese that I should be served in the dining room. The name Senhora punctuated her flurries of protest. But I insisted on staying where I was, and in the end a chair was drawn up for me beside the maids, and I consumed my eggs and tea and toast with relish. MacGregor had not spoken, but once I had caught his rheumy eyes fixed on me with an expression of what I thought, for him, might be amusement.

Now I stood in the first of the five rooms in which the collection was kept, staring at the ninth item on the list, which was a landscape painting by Fernandes. Lady Stewart had designated the rooms in which each treasure was to be found by a letter, and in order that there would be no mistake, she had drawn a sketch of the five rooms, the chapel, and the long gallery on the back of the first sheet. Her descriptions were quite clear. By eleven I had checked off every item except five; those five things, as far as I could determine, were not in the places where they should have been.

There was no possibility of my doing more than make a rough estimate of the value of what was gone. Besides the snuffbox, I could not find a small painted panel by Lopes which Lady Stewart had described as being a representation of the death of the Virgin. Also missing were two fourteenth-century bronzes of saints and a ruby ring that was supposed to have belonged to Dona Constanza, a Castilian who had been married to Don Pedro, the heir of Alfonso IV. Every one of the missing things was small, small enough to be taken from these rooms while tucked under a sweater or placed in a pocket. I guessed that the total worth of what was gone might be about ten thousand pounds—not, of course, if it had to be sold secretly. At an open auction such as those at Christie's, however, ten thousand pounds was a modest estimate.

There was no question in my mind but that I must let Lady Stewart know, and it struck me as somehow wrong to send a note until I was certain that Senhora was determined to prevent me from seeing her. Tucking the checked list into the pocket of my blouse, I left the dimly lit rooms of the wing by way of the long gallery and crossed the sunlit courtyard to the side door of the main house, refusing to think of the beauty of the place by moonlight and the eagerness with which I had left my room to meet David in the shadow of the white walls.

I could hear a man's voice speaking beyond the door of
Lady Stewart's bedroom, and my first thought was that the
doctor was with her. But when Senhora opened the door
to me, I saw Martin Kubler standing by the canopied
bed. His broad face was set in sober lines as he bent over
Lady Stewart, who, no longer propped high on her pillows,
lay flat on the bed, her body muffled by layers of thick
blankets. He raised his eyes to meet mine, and for the first
time I saw him as a man in himself, an individual. The
resemblance to Philip no longer struck me, perhaps because under no circumstances could Philip have managed
to convey, as Martin did, the impression of quiet
command.

"So it's you!" Senhora hissed as I closed the door behind me. She was wearing the same crumpled skirt she
had worn the day before, and the same shabby sweater
was bunched about her leanness. Her dark skin was even
darker under her eyes, and her face was molded in hard
lines.

"Have you come to see the damage you've done?" she
demanded. "She's unconscious. See for yourself."

I moved slowly across the long room to the bed. The
drapes of the long windows were drawn; it could have been
midnight outside. The same small lamp cast an oval of
light over the gray face of the old woman. Her eyes were
closed, and she was breathing heavily.

"You were here last night, weren't you?" Senhora asked
accusingly from behind my shoulder. "Don't deny it. I
heard you leave the room. I watched you leave with my
own eyes. It's no good MacGregor trying to lie about it—
or you, either."

Ignoring her, I spoke across the bed to Martin Kubler.
"What's happened?" I asked in a low voice.

He had been holding the old woman's wrist, but now
he placed her arm gently on the blanket. The light from
the bedside lamp fired the red of his hair as he raised

his head. His eyes met mine. "I want to speak to you for a moment, Miss Haverlock," he said.

"Irene," I murmured. Somehow I did not want to maintain the fiction that I was a stranger to him. No one who could arouse such strong responses of confidence in me could ever be a stranger. I went with him to a shadowy corner of the room, not aware, until she spoke, that Senhora had followed us.

"Don't let this woman lie to you," she said shrilly, pointing a finger at me. "I told her that it would not be possible for her to speak directly with Lady Stewart. She is responsible for this."

"Be quiet!" Martin spoke in a low voice, but there was no mistaking the absolute nature of the command, the command of a doctor accustomed to dealing with people who followed orders, at least in the sickroom. "I intend to talk to Miss Haverlock in private. As for you, it would be best if you sit by Lady Stewart. I should be informed if there is any change in her condition. Is that clear?"

"It is not for you to give orders!" Senhora spat out the words. "I will not be treated——"

"If you find it impossible to control yourself," Martin Kubler said, "perhaps it would be better if one of the maids watches her. We can send to Oporto for a professional nurse. Yes, on the whole, I think that would be best."

For a moment the dark woman glared at him, and then she turned and stalked across the room to the bed.

"Perhaps," Martin Kubler murmured, "it would be better, under the circumstances, if we talked outside." In a loud voice he said to Senhora: "I'll be in the corridor if you need me."

She made no response, nor did he speak to me until we were outside the door. A maid was dusting the statue behind which I had hidden the night before, but on seeing us, she scuttled down the corridor. It was better here in the full light that poured in at the long window at the end of the passage. I was not sorry to have left the bedroom and Senhora behind me.

"First of all," Martin said in a low voice, "I should explain why I'm attending Lady Stewart this morning. I realize that after what was said at the luncheon table the other day, you may find my presence in her bedroom somewhat irregular."

He was the sort of person whose eyes address you as directly as their voice. "No," I said. "After all, you're a doctor, and Lady Stewart is ill."

"She has a regular doctor," he reminded me, "and technically, I'm a psychiatrist. The fact remains that you must wonder why her regular doctor hasn't been called in."

I found that I could not play a hedging game with this man, even under the guise of politeness.

"Yes," I said, "I did wonder."

He smiled as though my frankness delighted him. "There's a simple-enough explanation," he said. "Lady Stewart's regular doctor lives in Oporto, which is a fair distance, and at the moment, he's ill. I'm a medical doctor as well as a psychiatrist," he said. "I'm quite qualified to attend her." He hesitated. "I know there's probably no need for me to try to justify my presence here, but I want you to understand that when I arrived—when I realized the situation for what it was—I wanted no part of it. I intended to leave Portugal today, to return to London. Under the circumstances I have no choice but to stay until another doctor is found who will be willing to come the distance from Oporto, or until Lady Stewart's own doctor recovers. He is, I understand, an elderly man who has been treating her for years."

It was all straightforward enough, and I found that I wanted to believe him. I had been a fool to let the atmosphere of mistrust in this house affect me. I instinctively trusted this man.

"How serious is her condition?" I said. "Senhora is

right, you know. I came to see Lady Stewart last night—very late—but it was at her request. If it's anything that I did——"

"No," Martin said gently. "I'm certain that you weren't responsible, but the thing is this: Apparently you were the last person to see her conscious. Senhora claims she found Lady Stewart in the state she is still in early this morning. Whatever you can tell me about her condition when you talked to her will be important."

I stared at the window reflectively. What was it that Senhora had said to me? That she had seen me leaving Lady Stewart's room the night before? If that was so, how did it happen that she had not gone directly to her mistress? I could not imagine her not doing so, and if she had, then I was not the last person to have seen her during the night.

"What's wrong, Irene?" Martin murmured. In the clear light that flooded us from the window I saw that his face was drawn. Obviously he was under a great deal of tension—and no wonder. The entire responsibility for this situation had been suddenly cast on his shoulders.

"Senhora found Lady Stewart unconscious, you say?" I asked him.

"Yes, this morning."

"She did not see her last night, after I had left the bedroom?"

"No. Or if she did, she saw fit not to tell me."

His eyes were brown like Philip's, but Philip had never looked at me in precisely the way this man was looking —as though he really saw me. Yes, that was exactly it. With Martin it was as though there were so much mutual understanding between us that we could talk on two levels at once. Perhaps it was because he was accustomed professionally to searching for the real person behind the mask, the real meanings in words strung one after the other. Whatever the reason, I knew that he would not misinterpret anything that I said. I decided not to pursue the subject of Senhora. Both of us realized that she might well prove a liar.

"When I left Lady Stewart," I said, "she seemed to be well enough. A bit tired, I think. I imagine that she found it a strain to talk, but there were certain things she felt that she should say to me. She coughed some while I was with her, and once I thought that she was in pain."

Martin nodded. "She's a dying woman, you know," he said.

"That was what I was told."

"She had a massive stroke a few months ago," he said. "That much is obvious. She's paralyzed from the waist down. Since then there have been other slight strokes. Fortunately—or unfortunately perhaps for her—the strokes have not affected her mind. There's heart damage as well. That's undoubtedly why she coughs a good deal."

"But—but how do you know about her mind?" I asked him. "You haven't talked with her since you arrived at Alcombra, have you? And she was already unconscious when you were called to her this morning."

"I confess that what I know about her mental condition is based on hearsay," Martin admitted. "You're quite right. I haven't talked with her. When William suggested that she see me, she refused. I'm basing my estimation of her lucidity on what her grandnephew told me."

"David?"

"Yes. Forget that I mentioned the state of her mind. I was brought here, as you probably know, because her stepson felt that her mind had been affected by the strokes. He claimed to have no faith in the doctor from Oporto. I had no idea when he talked to me in London that there was a question of vested interest on his part. I mean I was not aware that he was interested in breaking her will on the basis of my testimony. You've talked with her. Did you find her rational?"

"Yes," I said, "completely rational. She had the feeling that she was losing her control over the household. I

think she may have felt that Senhora deliberately intended
to keep her from any contact with anyone besides herself, but I think she had good reason for feeling that way."

"Yes," he said. "I sense something. . . ."

For a moment he was silent, staring past at the window,
his broad face intent with concentration. He was, I
thought for no reason, taller than Philip. My head was
level with his shoulder. But it was not a matter of small
differences. There was something solid about this man,
something unutterably reassuring.

"It would be best," he said, almost as though he were
talking to himself, "if she were in a hospital. I think that
she's suffered another slight stroke, but I can't be certain.
Senhora tells me that she's always refused to consider
leaving Alcombra. However, I don't think that I can take
the responsibility. I'll be honest with you, Irene, I want
to leave this place as soon as possible."

I felt a sudden unreasoning shock of anxiety and
realized that for some reason I did not completely understand myself, I did not want him to go.

"And you," he said, his eyes meeting mine, "are you
quite certain that you should stay?"

It was as though a tape recorder had been set off in my
mind. I seemed to hear Lady Stewart's voice telling me
that she trusted me.

"No," I said. "I can't explain why, but I feel that I
must stay."

To my surprise, lunch was brought to me on a tray
while I worked in the small chapel. The maid muttered
something about Senhora having said that I should have
my midday meal here in the future and disappeared. I was
glad enough of the chance to continue my work uninterrupted by a foray into the main house, but at the same
time I found it rather strange that Senhora had changed
her mind—unless she wanted to keep me away from the
others as much as possible. The night before, when I

had come upon her and William Stewart, she had dropped the fact that she knew Marian and I had talked together. She had gone further than that, actually, implying that I was helping Marian—whatever that was supposed to mean. Senhora had obviously determined to keep me as much as possible away from the others as well.

Whatever her motives in having given the order, I had no complaint. I did not want to see David again so soon. There was little room in my mind now for anything except the necessity of finishing the inventory as soon as possible. I wanted to be certain beyond any doubt that those parts of the collection which I had not been able to find were, indeed, missing. If there actually was a thief in the house, the knowledge that I was listing the contents of the rooms could act only as a preventive to further theft —assuming always that Lady Stewart's memory had not played her false, that she had had in her possession the ring and the painted panel and the other things I had not been able to find. It occurred to me that since she was not able to take steps to prevent anyone but me from entering these rooms, perhaps I should do so. The wing did not appear to be locked, either at night or at any other time. There had been no necessity to give me keys to these rooms. Even the first time I had come here, everything had been open, vulnerable to anyone who might wish to come here. Yet all the rooms had locks. I determined to talk to MacGregor that night and see that this part of the house was protected. Surely that would have been the order that Lady Stewart would have given.

I sat on the small altar beside an elaborately carved fourteenth-century lectern and ate the lunch of cold meat and salad. A carafe of rosé had been provided, and I sipped it slowly, lost in thought, while beyond the stained-glass windows the afternoon light faded. A shower was evidently approaching, for I heard the crack of distant thunder.

The question of the missing pieces of the collection

was, I found, beginning to obsess me. It was reasonable to suspect theft—only too reasonable, considering the situation. William Stewart needed money if what David had told me was true. There was every chance that he would not be able to invalidate his stepmother's will after her death. David had implied that he was an unscrupulous man. It would not have taken any particular creativity on his part to have come up with the idea of safeguarding his future by taking what he could from this wing. If that was true, he must have been upset when he had discovered that I had been hired to do the inventory. Certainly Marian had made no secret, during that first day's drive here with me, that she was opposed to the idea. She had subsequently admitted to me that she had for a long time grudged the fact that none of Lady Stewart's wealth had been shared with her side of the family. William had an even more direct claim in that it had been his father's money that had allowed the collection to be accumulated in the first place. Either one of them could have easily formulated a rationale that would have excused their taking what they wanted.

But, I reminded myself, pouring out the last of the wine, it was scarcely fair to restrict the list of suspects to Marian and William Stewart. The house was full of people, not only guests but servants. Senhora had told William that she would not be party to an attempt to prove Lady Stewart mentally incompetent, but would she have necessarily rejected the opportunity to help herself to a few small objects of art while she still had the opportunity? Perhaps, when Lady Stewart saw my final list, she would realize that many more of her possessions than five were missing. Perhaps someone had been helping himself for years. I knew nothing about MacGregor, for example, except that Lady Stewart had trusted him to keep us uninterrupted the night before. Still, it might be that the old man could be depended upon to do anything that would foil Senhora. There was likely to be a certain amount of rivalry between two long-term retainers such as they were.

It was all hypothesis, however. I put the tray aside and rose, reminding myself that it was too early for accusations. I could try to see to it that the wing was locked in the future, but other than that my only responsibility was to complete the inventory. Luckily the chapel was not going to take much time. Most of the objects were large, like the sarcophagus and the altar screen.

The thunder was closer now, and the light was so dim that I had to turn on all the small electric tapers and use the flashlight as well. Usually the air in the rooms where I was working was cooler than outside because of the thickness of the stone walls, but as the storm approached, the atmosphere became more and more oppressive. The silence, which until now I had welcomed, seemed somehow ominous.

I was intent on reading the Latin inscription at the base of a small twelfth-century statue of the Virgin when I heard the sound. For a moment I thought it was simply the cracking of the thunder, and then I heard it again and realized that someone was walking about in one of the adjoining rooms. I got to my feet and went to the door, and as I did so, the sound unmistakably became that of heels clicking on the tiled floor.

My first thought was that the maid had returned to take the tray back to the kitchen, but then I realized that all of the servants, with the exception of MacGregor, Senhora, and the housekeeper, wore cork-soled native sandals. I stood in the arched stone doorway that Lady Stewart had brought from God knows what decaying country chapel and stared into the next room. The lights were not on there, and I could see only shadows, all of them immobile in the dusk.

In order to switch on the lights in the room I would have to cross to the other side, and the idea held no appeal for me. Thunder rumbled overhead, and the room was plunged into deeper darkness. Rain began to splatter against the stone grilled windows set high in the walls.

I waited, uncomfortably aware that I was afraid. It was the kind of fear I had known as a child when my parents had put me to bed in the room on the third floor of the town house in Chelsea where we had lived, a room that was part of an old nursery, with iron bars on the small windows and deep dark corners and closets. I remembered how my heart had pounded as I had huddled under the covers, casting reason aside, certain that someone was in the room with me, plugging my ears so that I could not hear them if they moved, pressing myself into the mattress, as though by some miraculous effort I could become part of the bed. Now the same feeling was rising in me, the same panic, the same certainty that I was not alone.

"Who's there?" My voice sounded harsh and unfamiliar to me. "Is anyone there?" There was no answer, no sound, until a thin white line of lightning ripped its way across that small portion of the sky visible from the window above me to the right.

I tried to will myself to move, to turn back to the chapel and continue my work. Or if I did not have the courage to stay here alone, I could go out through the long gallery and cross the courtyard to the house. Run away. I taunted myself with the words.

No, I would stay. It was only three in the afternoon, and I had another good three hours' work ahead of me. With any luck, I could finish the chapel today, and that would leave me with only the five rooms—the hardest rooms to deal with, granted. But the psychological value of having done the long gallery and the chapel in the first two days would be valuable.

The detailed remembrance of what I had already done and what I meant to do gave me confidence. Tomorrow I would lock this wing off from the rest of the house not only during the day but also when I was working here. The maid could leave the luncheon tray outside the door at a certain time. I need never go through this particular experience again if I could be given the keys, and even if Lady Stewart did not regain consciousness soon, I was certain that MacGregor would give them to me.

In the meanwhile I could reassure myself by beaming the flashlight around this room—reassure myself and go back to translating the inscription, which would give me a more positive identification of the Virgin. It was as simple as that. The flashlight was in my hand. How strange that it should be necessary for me to literally force myself to move my finger over the switch. Suddenly it was done, and a pool of light shone on the tiled floor. I raised the torch abruptly and sent it scanning about the crowded room, flickering over the hooded fireplace, the cabinets, the statues. Everything the light touched seemed to be given a life of its own as it was propelled out of the darkness, and then there was a face peering out at me, a black-mustached man with cruel eyes and a ruff. . . .

I heard myself laugh shrilly as I realized that it was only one of the portraits that lined the walls. The laugh rebounded off the stone walls and seemed to flood against my ears, and over the echo I heard another laugh—that of a man—and something inside me seemed to freeze. I lowered the flashlight, my arm gone weak, and Jerez Caravels stepped into the glare. His teeth glittered in his swarthy face.

"I must apologize," he said. "I think, perhaps, that I have frightened you."

I turned my back on him and went into the chapel, where the electric tapers made spots of light in the dusk. Overhead the thunder growled to a crescendo of discordant sound. I leaned against the stone wall, aware that my legs were shaking so that I could scarcely stand. Out of the corner of my eyes I saw Jerez standing in the arched doorway. I turned to face him.

"Why didn't you answer me when I called?"

"You must accept my apologies, Miss Haverlock," he said, coming to take my arm. "Irene. Here, there must be somewhere you can sit down."

I let him lead me to the altar and sat down, clasping my hands about my knees to keep them from trembling. Relief was succeeded by anger. He had no right to frighten me as he had done. There was no reason. . . .

"It was the storm that brought me here," he said, sinking down beside me, pinching the crease in his trousers in that same gesture I had noticed in the courtyard when we had first met. He was wearing a gray lounge suit and a white shirt and tie. There was something foppish about the way he dressed—foppish and at the same time oddly old-fashioned. His elegance had amused me before, but now I found it annoying. He had lost my indulgence by standing silent in the shadows as I flashed the light around that room.

"The storm?" I said coldly.

"Ah, you are annoyed. I guessed that you *would* be annoyed at being disturbed. That was why I did not answer you when you first called. I thought that I could simply creep away. . . . Forgive me. It would have been much better for me to have identified myself at once and left you to your work, as I intend to do now. I realize, you see, better than the others that you must be left alone. It was I who encouraged Senhora to send you your luncheon here. I——" He was on his feet, moving toward the door.

"Why did you come here in the first place?" I demanded. "What has the storm to do with it?"

He smiled down at me. "It is only right," he said, "that under the circumstances I satisfy your curiosity. No, don't look at me like that. You terrify me."

He laughed again, but uneasily this time. The thunder and lightning seemed to have ceased, but the rain dashed heavily against the stained-glass windows.

"It's very simple, really," Jerez said. "When it started to rain, I was outside in the courtyard, and I happened to look over at this wing of the house and thought—thought, mind you, that I saw one of the windows open. Naturally I imagined the kind of damage that any sort of seepage might do, and so I came in here. I could hear you moving about in the chapel here, but as I said, I didn't want to disturb you. I'm making that my campaign, you see, to guarantee that you not be disturbed in your work."

He smiled down at me confidently, and I, in turn, looked down at the stone floor. It was a lie, of course. Did he expect that I did not know that it was improbable that any of those heavily grilled windows could be opened? He was here for some other purpose, and yet I found I could not challenge him. It was not that I was afraid. I simply sensed that it would be unwise to press the point. Something else lay under that smooth, smiling mask that this man presented to the world, but I did not want to know what it was.

"But, of course, I should have realized that you would be frightened when you heard me moving about," he went on. "It's a bit—eerie in here, don't you think? And then, of course, there was the thunder. The peacocks don't like it, you know—storms. I expect you heard them screaming a few minutes ago."

I felt as though his eyes were burning my face. I rose and went to the sarcophagus, running my hand over the alabaster fingers of the boy's effigy. "No," I said slowly. "I didn't hear the peacocks."

"I thought you might have." He took my arm, and it was all that I could do to keep myself from pulling away. "Am I forgiven, then?"

I forced myself to look at him. "Of course," I said.

"Then I will leave you to get on with your work," he said. "I must find Marian, at all events. I haven't seen her all this afternoon, and she's terrified of storms, you know —positively terrified. No, don't see me out. I can find my way. One is always afraid, of course, in these rooms that one will knock over some absolutely priceless piece of bric-a-brac, but there's more light now." He paused at the arched door. "Yes, the storm must be passing. Go on with your work. Believe me, my dear, I'll find some way to make amends for this unpardonable interruption."

I waited until I was certain that he was back in the main house, and then, flashlight in hand, I went through each of the five rooms, switching on the lights as I went. It was only by chance that in the last room, as I turned to go back to the chapel, I happened to see Marian Russell's body wedged behind a fifteenth-century coat of arms.

CHAPTER

5

At first I thought that for some reason Marian was hiding there. I actually spoke her name before I realized that her eyes were not focused on me but set in death. Lines of blood criss-crossed the wrinkled face, and her mouth hung open as though she were about to utter one last terrified protest.

I suppose I must have screamed. I remember only the sound of running feet, and suddenly the room seemed to be full of people. The body was being pulled out from its hiding place, the arms and legs limp as a puppet's. Someone laid her on the tiled floor, and I saw the blood-matted hair about the crushed skull. Then Martin Kubler was bending over the body, and someone's arms were about me, someone's hand shielding my eyes.

"What's happened?" David murmured.

"I switched on the lights, and she was there," I gasped. "Oh, my God! What happened to her?"

"Marian!" It was Jerez's voice. I saw him come through the door and push aside one of the staring maids.

"She's dead," Martin said as Jerez knelt, white-faced, beside the body. "Someone's beaten her skull in."

"No!" Jerez protested. "No! That can't be true!"

"Someone had better call the police," Martin said quietly. I glanced at him with gratitude. Something about his tone took an element of the horror away from the situation. A woman was dead. The police must be called. Terror would retreat, step by step. "Where's Mac-Gregor?" Martin continued.

The old man detached himself from the group and started toward the door, shuffling as always, his face set in what appeared to be an expression of grim satisfaction.

"Call the police and tell them there's been a murder and that they should get up here right away," Martin called after him. "The rest of you get out of this room. Nothing should be disturbed. I'm sorry, Mr. Caravels, but you must go, too. You can't do her any good now."

I fastened my eyes on Martin, drawing strength from him.

"He puts everything into perspective, doesn't he?" David said bitterly, but he kept his arm about me. We turned toward the door just as Claire stepped inside. She was looking more beautiful than usual in a pale-blue linen dress, her blond hair hanging loose about her shoulders.

"What's going on?" she asked, her voice shrill. "I thought I heard someone say. . . ."

Then she saw Marian's body. I suppose I expected her to react as violently as I had done, but she simply stared down at what was lying on the floor, her face expressionless. Behind her William hove into sight. It was he who cried out, and I saw her whirl to silence him by pressing the tips of her fingers to his mouth.

"If everyone will leave . . ." Martin Kubler said again, helping Jerez to his feet. The broad-boned Celtic face

of the man who had been Marian's fiancé was twisted
in a mask of grief. In the doorway he turned to me.

"Why did you do it to her?" he demanded.

"Are you insane, man?" David snapped, tightening his
arm about me.

"She was found in this room, wasn't she?" Jerez
cried hysterically. "I was here only a few minutes ago
looking for her and——"

"I thought you were looking for an open window," I
said in a low voice.

Jerez ignored me. I had the sense that he quite literally
did not know what he was saying.

"Irene Haverlock was the only person in here," he
said. "I went through all the rooms. If Marian was killed
here, she must have done it."

"Miss Haverlock may have been the only person here
when you came into the wing," Martin Kubler said, "but
if that was only a few minutes ago, as you say, it proves
nothing. It's my professional opinion that Miss Russell
has been dead for a matter of hours. Now, everyone out
into the hall, please. I'm going to see about locking this
room at both ends until the police arrive. That's right,
outside."

Propelled by the authority in his voice, we all crowded
out into the corridor that led to the main part of the
house. MacGregor sood waiting for us. I heard him
mutter something I did not catch, and three maids
scurried past him and disappeared.

"Did you call the police?" Martin demanded.

The old man nodded.

"Good. The next thing are the keys. I want to lock this
room."

Slowly the old man reached into a pocket of his rusty-
black suit and brought out an immense bunch of big
old-fashioned keys. Detaching two with great deliberate-
ness, he handed them to Martin.

"I want to stay with her," Jerez said in a shrill voice. "We can't just leave her in there alone."

"You can't do her any good now," Claire Stewart said in a hard voice.

"She's quite right, you know." The bluster in her husband's voice was only a thin echo of his usual heartiness. "Come along. What we all need is a drink."

For the first time since I had come to Alcombra, there was no talk of wine. In the long drawing room, with its broad windows draped in green-velvet hangings, William poured out Scotch for all of us. Martin Kubler joined us immediately, and we sat in silence in a semicircle of chairs and wide old-fashioned sofas around an empty fireplace lined with green tiles. I had not been in this room before, and to steady myself, I studied the paintings that lined the oak-paneled walls. Snatches of watery gray light illuminated two Vandykes, a Gainsborough, and several watercolors by Constable. I guessed that this room reflected the taste of Lady Stewart's husband, for everything in it down to the smallest cabinet reflected British craftsmanship and artistry. It was absurd, perhaps, to attempt to pretend to myself that I was back in London, with this horror behind me, but I did—until Jerez began to talk again.

"I told her that she ought to leave," he said. His voice was low now, even. He drained his glass, and William Stewart rose to pour him another drink. "She laughed at me when I said there was something wrong in this house. I sensed it from the first." His dark eyes fastened on me. "I'm sorry that I said what I did about you, Irene," he said. Then he laughed with a sudden wildness. "I seem to have spent a good deal of my time today apologizing to you."

"The thing we've got to think about," Claire said in a clear voice, "is making it quite clear to the police that none of us could have been responsible for this—this thing."

She was sitting on one of the two sofas that faced one another in front of the open mouth of the fireplace. As she spoke, she tucked her legs under her and looked around at us with clear, untroubled eyes.

"I doubt whether it will be as easy to do that as you may think, my dear," her husband said, handing Jerez his drink and coming to sit heavily beside his wife.

"Nonsense!" Claire snapped. "It should be quite obvious that none of us could have done such a—such an uncivilized thing."

"Who would you suggest, then?" David asked her. He was sitting on a footstool at my feet. I could not see his face, but his voice was hard and unwavering. Still, I knew that he more than any of us, except possibly Jerez, was torn to shreds inside. Despite his alienation from his mother, he had cared for her—cared, perhaps, more than he had realized until this moment. Martin's pragmatism might have reassured me, but there was no reassurance for David—only the agony of loss. I knew that he could not trust his own reactions. Thus the hardness in his voice. Perhaps it was asking too much to think that Claire could realize what he was going through.

"Of course, you can't be expected to be completely rational about this right now," Claire said brightly. "After all, I suppose, she *was* your mother."

"She was as much a stranger to me as you are," David said.

"That simply isn't true," Claire said vivaciously. Having taken the stage, it was clear that she intended to captivate us all. "You might not have seen her since you were a child, but she was your mother. Martin will tell you that certain strong emotional ties——"

"I think, my dear . . ." Her husband began, patting her knee.

"What I'm trying to say," Claire went on, flashing him an angry look, "is that one of the itinerant workmen who are helping with the harvest must have done it. Remember when you took me around the vineyards the other day, William? I told you that they looked like a very shifty lot."

"That's absurd, my dear," her husband said heavily. "Those men are never anywhere near the house. They're lodged well over a mile away, and they would have no reason to come here under any circumstances. The vineyard and the house itself have been kept entirely separate since my father died."

"It's common knowledge that your stepmother has a valuable collection," Claire snapped. "Now, you can't deny that, William. Anyone could have gone into the wing hoping to steal something—not necessarily the workmen but, well, anyone. Any stranger. Probably Marian surprised whoever it was as he was taking something, and he killed her. It's quite a logical explanation, and——"

"Shut up, Claire!" At first I could not believe it was William Stewart speaking. His face was deeply flushed, and he was breathing heavily. "For God's sake, shut up! You don't know anything about any of this."

"She knows as much as any of us, I suppose," Martin Kubler said easily. The man had been slow in formulating any sort of distinct personality as far as I was concerned, but I had sensed an inner strength in him when we had talked earlier today outside Lady Stewart's bedroom, and now I realized that we might very well all come to depend on him for our stability in what was to come. The feeling of numbness which had crept over me after the first shock of seeing Marian's body was wearing away now. When Jerez had leveled his accusation at me, I had scarcely taken it in. The only thing that had meant anything to me in those first few minutes of recognition that a murder had, in fact, been committed had been the protection of David's arm. All the antagonisms of the night before on the hillside had fallen away—for him, I thought, as much as for me. He was no longer touching me, and yet I knew that he realized that I needed him close to me.

And so, for me, Claire's outburst meant little. I could rely on Martin Kubler and David to provide some sort of perspective on what had happened. I reached out and touched David's shoulder, and he turned and smiled at me.

"The first thing that I think we ought to agree on is that this should be kept from Lady Stewart as long as possible," Martin said. His voice was calm. I had never been more aware of the fact that he was a doctor, accustomed to dealing with crises of this sort. "I don't know whether you all realize that she had a stroke during the night—a slight stroke, I think, because she was conscious and rational when I left her an hour ago. But I doubt whether this would be the right time to subject her to any sort of shock."

Claire laughed bitterly. "From what I hear," she said, "I think she might find it a relief to know that there was one less of us to bother about."

Jerez muttered something unintelligible, and I saw William Stewart's hand close firmly over his wife's knee.

"I don't know why we shouldn't be frank," Claire protested. "Surely even Mr. Caravels realizes that all of us are unwanted guests."

"Be that as it may," Martin Kubler interrupted, "I think we can agree that Lady Stewart should not be told. The next thing to consider—and consider seriously—is that the police will undoubtably ask us a considerable number of questions. I would suggest that all of us stick to the facts as we know them and avoid any sort of verbal surmising as to what may or may not have happened."

"I can't see any reason why we shouldn't give them our opinions," Claire said stiffly, sweeping her hair back from her face. "I shall certainly tell them that I think they would do well to question the workmen—and to see if anything is missing from the collection."

"All else aside, my dear," William Stewart said wearily, "if the murderer was a thief, there would be no way of telling whether anything is missing or not, except in the unlikely event that my stepmother should be well enough to be brought down to the room herself. And even then —" he made a sweeping gesture with one arm—"even then I doubt very much if she could remember the exact location of every item. Even when she was well, I think that there were times when she was not certain what she had purchased and what she simply had meant to purchase."

"There's always Irene's inventory," David said in a low voice.

"Ah," William said ponderously, "but Irene hadn't inventoried that room yet, had she?"

"I don't know," David said evenly, "but I'd be interested in knowing how you reached that conclusion— unless she told you."

The fat man shifted restlessly on the sofa, his thick fingers fumbling with the buttons of his blue blazer. His small eyes darted toward me and away. "Actually—" he began—"actually——"

"I don't have any record of what was in that room," I said flatly. "I completed a list of the paintings in the long gallery yesterday, and I was working in the chapel this afternoon."

Claire laughed and curled herself more tightly into the corner of the sofa. "Poor William," she said, "you're always putting your foot in it, aren't you, darling?"

"Tell me, Miss Haverlock," Martin Kubler said abruptly. "Were you working in the wing during the entire day?"

"Yes," I said. "My lunch was sent to me there. I started work at seven this morning, and except for the few minutes that I spoke with you. . . ."

I broke off. I could have been mistaken, but I thought that his eyes flashed me a warning.

"And you say that during that time you were in the

chapel?" He stressed the last word as though he had mis-
understood me.

"We're forgetting that Martin here hasn't had a chance
to make the grand tour," William Stewart said heartily.
"Yes, she said 'chapel'—a little something my stepmother
had brought stone by stone from some place south of
Lisbon. My father put up with most of her nonsense, but
he nearly drew the line at that."

I stared at Martin Kubler curiously over the top of
David's blond head. Had Martin, I wondered, made a
deliberate point of the fact that he had not yet seen the
collection? This was in all probability true, however, because yesterday, during luncheon, Claire had suggested
taking him to see it. For a moment I remembered vividly
the way Jerez had interrupted to make the point that I
should be the one to act as guide.

"All that doesn't matter," Jerez said impatiently to William Stewart, who was still rambling on about the role of
his stepmother as scavenger. "The thing is, if Irene was
there all day——"

"Except for the 'few minutes' she was with Martin,"
Claire said sarcastically.

"That was in the morning," the doctor said flatly. "If
you'll remember, Miss Russell was at lunch. We are concerned with what happened in the five hours between
then and now."

"I wanted Marian to go for a walk with me," Jerez said,
rising and going to the liquor cabinet. I noticed that his
voice was slurred. "But she said that she was tired. She
wanted to take a nap. I could have insisted that she
come with me." His voice broke. "Something was bothering her. I could tell. . . ."

He broke off, the bottle of Scotch in his hand, as the
double doors to the drawing room were flung open and
Senhora appeared, her hair, loosened from its knot,
straggling on her swarthy cheeks. She was breathless, as

though she had been running, and her dark eyes seemed to be starting out of her face.

"What are the police doing here?" she asked. "Who called them? What do we want with the police? She was an old woman. Everyone knew that she was going to die."

There was no time after Senhora's announcement to gauge the immediate effect of the news on those of us gathered in the drawing room. MacGregor showed the police inspector into the room on Senhora's heels, and even she kept silent as the inspector doggedly explained to us in heavily accented English that it would be necessary for him to be shown the body at once, and that he would hear what we had to say afterward.

"Bodies," Claire said brightly, "in the plural." The inspector—a slight, weary-looking man with sunken cheeks and bloodshot eyes behind thick gold-rimmed spectacles —asked her to explain with a flatness that quelled Claire instantly, whereupon the little man, whose name it later developed was Soria, listened to what she had to say with the attitude of having expected something of this sort. One had the feeling that life was constantly playing this kind of trick on him: two dead women instead of one, a talkative young Englishwoman who preened herself as she rattled on interminably. Even Senhora, standing trembling with God knows what pent-up passions, did not escape his notice. When he heard enough of what Claire had to say, he left, and through the open door I saw three policeman standing awkwardly in the wide hall, one of them, the youngest, staring up at the painted ceiling with a gaping mouth. Then MacGregor shuffled into view in the hall, and the inspector moved forward to speak to him. Orders were obviously being transmitted. We watched in silence as one man was sent upstairs in the company of a white-faced maid, and the inspector and the other two policemen disappeared in the direction of the wing in MacGregor's wake.

If the situation had been awkward before, it was impossible from that point on. Martin left the room at once, pausing by the door to snap some questions at Senhora, who was still trembling, her sweatered arms crossed about her chest, apparently incapable of making him coherent answers. Martin slammed the doors behind him, and I realized that under the circumstances he had no choice but to go up to Lady Stewart's room to verify her death.

But I did not doubt that what Senhora had said was true, nor, I think, did the others. David was silent, his hands clenched between his knees. Jerez put down the bottle of Scotch without pouring himself another drink and stood rubbing his face with his hands and staring out one of the long windows at the wet lawns that rolled away from the house, gray under a glowering sky. A wind had begun to rise, and the pine trees that bordered the lawn were waving their boughs as though in an attempt to ward off the gathering storm. Claire uncurled herself from the sofa and started toward Senhora with the obvious intention of questioning her, but William heaved himself after her and led her, protesting, from the room.

As the doors closed behind them, Jerez appeared to make some sort of decision. Going to Senhora, he took her arm and led her to a chair.

"Marian is dead," he said simply. "Murdered."

I was not sure that the woman was able to take in what he said, but she refused the offer of a drink by shaking her head so violently that what was left of the bun tumbled loose in disheveled greasy strands about her face.

"The other was murder, too," she hissed, staring at David and me with eyes that did not quite come into focus. "Someone was in that room with her before she died."

"I thought that you were watching her," I said. As always the only emotion she aroused in me, even now when she was obviously distraught, was anger. I tried to keep my voice even. "Dr. Kubler told you to stay with her."

"I was only in my room for a few minutes," she said shrilly. "Someone must have been watching, someone who wanted her to die."

"You'd better make it clear exactly what you're saying," David said, rising from the footstool and jamming his fists into the pockets of his wrinkled slacks. "You mentioned murder. Are you saying that someone killed her—beat her head in, perhaps—as they did my mother?"

Jerez made a sound deep in his throat and covered his face with his hands.

"They may as well have done!" Senhora cried. "She's just as dead as if they had."

"Listen," David said with an ominous mildness, "are you trying to tell us that Lelia was attacked?"

"I don't know!" Senhora spat at him. "I only know that she is dead."

There was a momentary silence, broken only by the beating of the wind against the long windows. The room was wreathed in shadows, shadows as dark and threatening as the clouds that shadowed the sky.

Bending over Senhora, David put his hands on her shoulders. His face was pale. "Were there any signs that she had died of anything but a natural death?" he asked, spacing his words as though he were speaking to a child. It was obvious to me that he was desperately trying to maintain his self-control. There were deep currents in this man. I had sensed that the night when we had sat together on the hillside. His emotions were strong and complex. He had loved and hated his mother. Even his relationship with his grandaunt had been ambiguous. But there was no doubt in my mind that he despised and mistrusted Senhora. I knew that in this moment he wanted to hurt her, and I also knew that if that thin thread of self-control snapped, he might do so. Unlike Martin, he was a passionate man, capable of great hatreds—and great loves.

Senhora pulled herelf away from him, her eyes glittering. For the first time I could really understand how much she loathed all of us.

"Are you even certain that she's dead?" David asked. "She was not breathing," Senhora said defiantly. "I held a mirror to her lips, and there was no pulse. I am a nurse. Do you not think that I am capable of telling when death comes?"

"Don't you think that it's probable that your grandaunt had another stroke?" I said quietly. I did not want David to go on with this interrogation. In some obscure way I wanted to protect him against himself.

"I think that it is very probable," he said grimly, turning to me. "I simply want to make this woman admit that she's making wild accusations, and this is not the time."

"Perhaps," I said in a low voice, "this is not the time for anything, even questions."

For a long moment our eyes met, and then I saw his face relax. He held out his hand to me then, and I went with him. As we reached the door, I heard Jerez say something to Senhora in a low voice. But I had no interest in what passed between them. In the storm-darkened hall, at the foot of the broad stairs, we met Martin, who told us, grim-faced, that it was true Lady Stewart was dead and that although under the circumstances he imagined the police would order an autopsy, he was satisfied it had, in fact, been a second stroke that had killed her.

I listened to him explain the case as he saw it and heard a clinical detachment in his voice which somehow horrified me. Yet why should it? An old woman was dead of a stroke. Implicit in what Martin was saying was that there was nothing unusual about it, nothing to wonder at. David asked questions. "Yes," Martin said, it was possible that a sudden shock could have killed her, but

it was obvious that he intended to take no part in specu-
lation. Why, I wondered, should I have expected anything
else of him? There was no reason why he should deal
with the matter in a more imaginative manner because he
was a psychiatrist and not simply a medical doctor. Still,
whatever the reason, his encounter with us left me angry
and frustrated.

David's response was to insist that I go with him to his
grandaunt's bedroom. David and I stood silent, looking
down at Lady Stewart's body as fingers of rain tapped
impatiently against the thickly draped windows. I had
mistaken Marian's staring death for life, but there was no
mistaking what I saw here. The corpse lay slumped side-
ways, the white head flung to the side of the sloping mound
of pillows as though she had made one last frantic
struggle against oblivion. The broad, coarse-featured face
seemed to have shrunk, and for the first time I could see
the fine body structure of the girl Sargent had painted
so long ago. An hour had passed since Senhora had burst
into the drawing room to tell us that the old woman was
dead, but on the orders of the police the body had not
been moved. On their orders, too, a policeman had been
stationed in the hallway outside the door. When David
and I had come into the room, the man had followed us,
protesting in rapid Portuguese. But David had ignored
him, and I had understood. It was necessary that David
see for himself that she was dead.

Fretful with the realization that the guard was not
willing to leave us alone with the body, I broke the suffocating silence. "I'm sorry, David," I said, "truly sorry."

He gave a half laugh, his eyes fixed on the waxen face
on the pillow. "Why should any of us be sorry?" he said
in a low voice. "She was dying—in pain, helpless. It's
better this way, although I suppose she would have enjoyed
hearing that my mother is dead. She always hated my
mother."

"Don't," I begged. "Don't torture yourself."

"We all torture one another," David said, "pretending
love where none exists. The only reason Lelia kept me
here was because it was a way of hurting someone else.
Yet my mother never really wanted me. She never made
any real effort to get me back, no matter what she may
have told you. All that she was interested in was the
money. All that either of them were interested in was
money and what it would buy." He turned to me, and
it was as though he were forcibly tearing his eyes away
from the dead woman on the canopied bed. "I suppose
that sounds a little too dramatic for you, doesn't it?" he
asked. "It's the sort of thing people don't say—particularly
not men. It's not the sort of thing that the admirable
Doctor Kubler would tell you."

"Who?"

He had taken me by surprise with his sudden transition.
Even the bitterness in his voice was disconcerting.

"Our friend the doctor," he said, "or should I say, 'Your
friend the doctor'?"

I looked at him in the dim light. "You're upset," I said.
"Whether you want to believe it or not just now, your
mother and your grandaunt meant a good deal to you."

"I'm not talking about me," David said in a low voice,
taking my arm. "I'm talking about you, Irene. You're
really not too interested in having people tell you the
straight truth, are you? When I said that neither my
mother nor my grandaunt was interested in anything but
money and what it would buy, I meant it. But a man like
Kubler wouldn't have offended you by speaking the
truth. That's my only point. I——"

"Don't be absurd," I interrupted him. "If you believe
something to be true, you should say it."

"Ah, but there's the rub," David said as though he
were talking to himself. "It's sometimes difficult to know
what *is* truth and what we simply want to believe. I suppose if Lelia had been happy in her marriage, she might
not have developed her passion for collecting things. She

wasn't that good a judge of quality, you know. You'll find there are a good many things in that hoard of hers that are worthless. She simply wanted things because if she had them, no one else could. It was the same with me. She wanted me because my mother pretended to want me."

"You've got to consider that you may not be being fair," I said quickly, "to them or to me." He was doing what he had done the night before on the hillside: going to extremes. First the blanket condemnation of two women whom, whether he knew it or not, he had loved and needed; then the unwarranted attack on Martin, which had involved the statement that I could not bear to hear people speak the truth. "From what your mother told me," I went on evenly, "she gave you up of her own accord when you were an infant."

"Not of her own accord," David said harshly. "She gave me up because she couldn't face society with me. It wasn't that easy, twenty-five years ago, being an unmarried woman with a bastard."

"Tell me," I said softly. "Did you talk to your mother before she died?"

He might have answered me, but at that moment the guard chose to accost us again, reminding us in rapid-fire Portuguese that we were not supposed to be in the room. He was the young man I had seen earlier staring at the ceiling in the hall below, and he waved his arms frantically in an attempt to make his point.

"All right," David muttered. "Let's get out of here. My God, when are they going to see to settling this? They can't just leave her like this indefinitely."

"Probably they have to wait for a coroner," I told him as we walked out of the dimness of the room into the corridor, where last long drops of rain were streaking the windows. Below us in the courtyard a peacock screamed, and I suddenly remembered Jerez asking me if I had heard them scream just before the storm began.

It occurred to me that what he might have heard was Marian screaming, but that was absurd. If she had cried out, I would have heard her—if she had been killed in the room in which her body had been found, that is. And that did not have to be the case. She could have been somewhere else, carried there, and hidden. Perhaps the murderer had hoped that since the wing was so unfrequented, she would not be found for some time. Still, he had been taking a chance. Everyone in the house, including the servants, had known that I was working there. I had heard Jerez moving about in the room next to the chapel. I might have heard the murderer as well—unless it was one and the same person, unless Jerez had killed her, and having hidden the body, deliberately alerted me, albeit in another room, with a feeble excuse about closing a window. But no. That did not make sense. I wanted desperately to think clearly, but my mind felt as though it were wrapped in cotton wool.

I realized that somehow we had reached the top of the broad staircase, and that David had stopped, putting out his hand as though in warning. Looking down past his shoulder, I saw the inspector and one of his men coming up the stairs, heads bent, not seeing us. Martin Kubler followed them, and behind him came another man, wearing a wrinkled white suit, a bald man with a few tufts of white hair standing up behind his ears.

"Quick," David whispered, "in here."

It was apparently his bedroom. A knapsack lay on the floor beside an old-fashioned brass-railed bed. It was a high-ceilinged, spacious room, but unlike mine, it was full of shabby, comfortable furniture, had a desk littered with papers, and was lined with bookcases. The windows were open, and two peacocks sat on one of the sills, craning their necks in our direction. David made a dash at them, waving his arms, and they disappeared with a flash of vividly colored tail feathers.

"Look," David said, turning back to me. "I wanted us

to have a chance to talk before we encounter the inspector again. It's my bet that the old fellow is the police doctor. They'll probably be holed up in Lelia's bedroom for a while, so we have time. Sit down."

I did as he said, passing a mirror and looking hastily away from my own reflection. My face was smeared with dirt, and my slacks were wrinkled. Suddenly I was uncomfortably aware of the fact that I had not even combed my hair since seven o'clock that morning. Suddenly I felt not only dirty but also exhausted, and yet I was glad that David and I had made our escape. I did not want to risk going to my own room just now if it meant risking an encounter with the police.

"It's just this," David said, dragging his easy chair close to mine. "Once they get started, the police are going to ask a lot of questions. They're going to want to know when you last saw my mother, for one thing."

"Not since yesterday evening," I said wearily, leaning my head back against the cushions and closing my eyes. It was strange how long ago yesterday could seem.

"And Lelia?"

"Last night—after I left you. MacGregor was waiting outside my door when I got back. She wanted to see me."

There was a long pause. I did not open my eyes. I wanted to believe that David was asking me these questions out of genuine concern for my protection from suspicion. If I looked at him, I knew that there was just a chance I would see something else in his eyes.

"What about?" he said in a low voice. "Tell me, Irene. What did she want to see you about?" I felt his hand on my arm. "Whoever else you lie to, don't lie to me—because I think we're in danger, you and me. Someone obviously believed that my mother had to die, and I don't believe that it's going to end there."

The thing that I could never explain to myself later was why I did not tell him about his grandaunt's fear that her collection might have been pillaged, nor did I tell him about the five items I had already found missing. It was not because I did not trust him; I think it was because there had been no time for me to think about the possibility of such thefts having been committed in the context of Marian's murder. Granted that Claire had suggested a relationship when she had spoken of the possibility of Marian's having surprised someone in the room where she had died. But Claire had been attempting to place the blame for murder on one of the workers in the vineyard, a stranger, and I did not think that was true.

So because I needed time to think about how I would deal with a knowledge that at present was only mine, I had told David that Lady Stewart had wanted to see me about the procedure the inventory would take, and that she had sent for me at the unlikely hour of midnight because she knew Senhora was opposed to having me in the house in the first place and wanted our talk to be undisturbed. I don't think he had believed me, but there had been no time for him to probe, because we had been interrupted by William Stewart, who had made it clear, in his heavy-handed way, that he wanted to talk to David alone about "family business."

I had gone to my room then, thinking that I would take a long bath and lie down for a while—and try to think. But on my way from David's room to my own, I had encountered two white-jacketed men carrying a stretcher, and I had been overcome by the feeling that this house and what was going on inside it were stifling me. The rain had cleared now, and when I opened a window, I smelled the fresh dampness of the earth. Pausing only long enough to shower and slip on a loose white-linen shift, I had run a brush through my hair and hurried out of the house past the ambulance waiting in the gravel drive.

Wondering where to go, I hurried to the west side of the house and stood in the shelter of a huge mimosa bush out of sight of anyone who might be looking out the drawing-room windows. There was the hill behind the house which I had climbed with David the night before, but I did not want to go there alone. Besides, there was always the possibility that if he decided to come looking for me when William was finished talking to him, he would look on the hill if he could not find me in my room.

The front of the house was lined with green turf, which stretched away into a park, the park through which we had driven the night I had come to Alcombra. I started in that direction but then changed my mind. There was too much chance that I would be seen leaving if I took that unprotected route, and besides, I suddenly remembered the way the car had brushed its way under the low limbs of the pine trees that crowded the narrow road that led up to the house. The rain would have made the trees wet and dripping.

I looked to the west again, to where the enveloping distant hills were turning purple in the first fading light of the sunset. The air was fresh and cool, and now that I was out of the house I already felt better. All that I needed to do was to walk for a while alone, and what better place to walk than westward, where the terraced vineyard faded into the hills?

Hurrying down the sloping lawn in the shelter of the shrubbery, I paused twice, once to turn aside to avoid one of the peacocks who fixed himself defiantly in front of me, his exotic feathers spread in a fan, and once more to look back at the house. The setting sun turned the long windows into panels of flame, which seemed to leap out from the gray stone. There was a brooding quality about the house, a quality that incorporated the ominous mood of what had happened there. A peacock screamed in the distance, and suddenly I seemed to see Marian's face, the mouth open in a cry of terror. Stumbling, I pushed my way through the hedges and found myself on a dirt path that led down into a bowl-like valley lined with terraced vines.

It was quiet here. To my left the granite wall that supported one of the terraces gave out the captured warmth of the day. To my right the ground fell away to the next terrace. Once when I had been a girl my father had taken me to visit a friend who lived in Bordeaux. His vineyards had been less extensive than this, but I remembered the absorption with which he had explained the complexities of wine-farming. In the autumn, as soon as the grapes were harvested, it was necessary to dig hollows around the vine trunks to catch the rain. "There is never enough rain," he had told my father, "except in those years when there is too much, and then the landslides. . . ." He had waved his arms in Gallic desperation, and I remembered how my father and I had smiled at one another.

Leaning against an outcropping of the granite wall, I let the fading warmth of the sun strike my face. It was odd how, quite suddenly, I could remember so much of that long summer day when I had walked with the two men among the vines, intrigued by the description of how blue lupine had to be sown between the rows of vines, of the process of careful pruning, the replanting, the grafting—and then at last, the vintage. Reaching up, I plucked a bunch of purple grapes off the vine and ate them, staring into the past. It was all so familiar, this moment— and so deceptive. Try as I might, I could not retreat into a time when all my decisions had been made for me, when security was as close as my father's hand.

I shook my head impatiently and continued to walk along the dirt path. I could not remember a time when I had not tried to escape reality when it became too unpleasant. It was a fault, and I knew it. Yet habit was strong. I had known that I did not want to marry Philip for months before the final break came, and in the end he had been the one who had had to make it, because rather than take a stand, I would retreat into the protection of the past or into dreams. He had called me a coward, and he had been right.

I stopped walking again and struck my hands together

impatiently. I was doing it again: first the memory of my father and then of Philip. One consoling, the other painful. But both were conjured up deliberately to keep me from thinking of Alcombra and violence and death.

Pulling myself up on the wall beside me, I sat and stared out over the valley. For the first time I noticed in the distance the red-tiled roofs of a string of low, barrack-like houses and heard from far away the faint sound of an accordion being played. That must be where the workers were housed, I realized—a long distance from the house. I remembered what Claire had suggested about one of the workers having attacked Marian. Even though they were in the fields during the day, closer to the house, I found that the idea of one of them coming in-side, particularly into the wing, to steal anything seemed absurd to me—certainly not in broad daylight. The risk would be too great. Besides, if the items I had checked off on Lady Stewart's list had been stolen, they had been stolen by someone who knew enough about the value of such things to have chosen items from the collection which, although small, were of great value. And David had been right when he had said that his great-aunt had accumulated a mass of bric-a-brac. I had seen enough of what was in those rooms to know that was true. Whoever had taken the ring and the panel and the rest had been someone of some degree of artistic discrimination.

Yet if that was true, who did that leave to suspect, even if one narrowed one's suspicions to the members of the household? Neither Marian nor David had ever mentioned anything that might indicate that he was interested in art. The same held true for Marian herself, and for Claire. William had obviously never taken any interest in what his stepmother collected. His only attitude toward her pos-sessions seemed to have been one of resentment, if what David had told me about him when he was still living at Alcombra was true. And David himself? His field was Georgian poetry. Certainly it did not follow that he

knew anything about Iberian art. In my talk with him he
had never mentioned a single one of Lady Stewart's
acquisitions. As for Martin Kubler, what did I know of
him except that he was a psychiatrist or claimed to be
a psychiatrist? He had expressed an interest in seeing the
collection, but surely that was only natural. Even Claire
had apparently seen it. I expected that every visitor to
Alcombra had at some time or other taken the grand
tour. Besides, Martin had been in the house for only a few
days. Or had he? It occurred to me that I did not know
exactly when he had arrived, even whether or not he had
accompanied William and Claire from London. I had
accepted him at face value because—because of the quiet
confidence of the man and because, from the very beginning, there had been a certain rapport between us. And
yet . . . and yet there were so many things I did not know.
In the end I ought to admit that I knew so little that
there was no use in my speculating over what had
happened.

But I was certain of one thing. Although I had not
chosen to tell David about the fact that certain parts
of the collection were missing, I would have to tell the
police if for no other reason than to ensure that the
wing be locked during the times I was not there, and that
the key be placed in safekeeping—even though it might
occur to them that I had ample opportunity to take what
was missing myself. Certainly I would rank high among
their suspects as a person who would know what was most
valuable, and therefore most worth stealing. It was, I
realized suddenly, entirely possible that once the police
knew of the thefts, they would not allow me to conclude
the inventory. I would simply have to convince them that
it was an essential step if Alcombra was to become a
museum.

But why did I have to do any such thing? Presumably
Lady Stewart's will provided for a particular procedure
that was to be followed after her death. Perhaps a curator

had already been appointed—someone who would immediately take over after the will was probated—but legal processes were slow. Even if William did not dispute the terms of the will, there was no question of the museum's being established within a few months—not even, perhaps, for years.

I pushed my hair back from my face. There was a cool breeze. The part of the vineyard that lay below me in the bowl of the hills was gray-green in the growing shadows. Only a sliver of the red sun showed above the distant hills. Back at the main house the police might be looking for me. The inspector had said that he would want to talk to all of us. It had been unwise, perhaps, for me to leave without telling anyone where I was going. I had to face the fact that Lady Stewart's death and the will, even the thefts, were secondary to the question of who had murdered Marian Russell.

They could not suspect me of that, at any rate. I had no reason to have wanted her dead. She was a stranger to me, as were all the people in that house. They would see that, surely. But what would they see as well? That David had a life-long reason to hate his mother? That perhaps Jerez had agreed to marry her under the impression that she was an heiress, and that this visit to Alcombra might have disillusioned him? But surely disillusionment alone would not have been an adequate reason for him to have murdered her. Still, they had been close to one another. There could have been other reasons for him to want her out of the way. What use was there in my thinking about it? I knew so little, and even that little was more than I wanted to know. Had it been only two days ago that I had so ruthlessly attempted to keep Marian from drawing me into this little world? This terrifying world.

I slid down from the wall and started slowly back toward the house. Far below me an accordion pulsed out a wailing song. The breeze rippled the leaves of the vines, and an unutterable sadness engulfed me. Lost in thought, I wandered up the dirt path, my eyes on the ground. It was only by chance that I heard something falling above me, only by chance that I stepped aside as the jagged granite missile plunged past me and lodged itself among the vines below.

CHAPTER

6

The inspector was, surprisingly enough, not willing to admit that anything unusual had happened to me. "There is a Douro saying," he told me. " *'Ano sem sapada, não da nada.'* Which means, 'A year without a landslide is a year that gives nothing.' Vineyard walls are always collapsing, particularly after such a rain as we had this afternoon. You were fortunate to avoid being hurt, Miss Haverlock, but I find it difficult to believe that that stone was dislodged deliberately. It is quite natural, you realize, after a murder has been committed for everyone to see danger in the corners, so to speak."

MacGregor had been waiting in the hallway at Alcombra when I had reached the house, breathless from having run all the way—breathless, perhaps, from panic as well. Because I had been certain when that piece of granite had shattered its way past me that someone wanted me to die, and that that someone was hidden above me, behind one

of the layers of walls. I had scarcely listened to Mac-
Gregor as he muttered something about someone—perhaps
the police—having looked for me. I had wanted only one
thing: to see the inspector and tell him what I knew—
everything I knew. I had left this house in order to think
about what I should do, how much I should tell. The piece
of falling granite had decided me. I would trust the police
and no one else.

I think I would have insisted on seeing the inspector
whether he had been waiting for me or not. He had set
up what seemed to be a sort of temporary office in a little
room toward the back of the house, a room that had
apparently been someone's study, perhaps Lady Stewart's
husband's. Whoever's refuge it had been, I had the feeling that it had not been used for a long time. There was
no dust, but there was something about the bareness of the
massive oak desk, something about the symmetry of the
books that lined the walls, which hinted at desertion.

I had not waited for the inspector to begin to question
me before I told him about what had just happened in
the vineyard. He had listened, puffing on a cigarette, his
thin, exhausted face illuminated by the white light of a
metal desk lamp. Then he had discounted the incident,
putting out the cigarette and lighting another, his dark
eyes never leaving my face.

He asked questions then—about my relationship to the
family, about the gallery in London, about what I was
doing here—chain-smoking all the while, leaning on the
desk in a manner that seemed to convey nothing but weariness and an incredible boredom. It was as though he had
been investigating Marian's murder for months instead of
a few hours, as though nothing that I could tell him would
come as a surprise. Even when I told him about the list
Lady Stewart had given me, and that some of the possessions seemed to be missing, there was no real reaction
on his part.

"Yes," he said. "That's very interesting, Miss Haver-

lock. I shall want to see that list, of course. We shall have
to ascertain whether or not those things are really missing.
As you say, they might simply have been misplaced. It is
quite possible that Lady Stewart did not remember their
location accurately."

"The collection should have been kept locked," I said.
Now that I had blurted out everything I knew that could
possibly be of any importance, I felt a great sense of relief.
It was as though I had conveyed a burden to someone
else—as, of course, I had. Yet there was no sense of re-
laxation. I sat on the edge of my chair across the desk
from him, tensely twisting my fingers together.

"Under ordinary circumstances one does not suspect
one's servants or the members of one's household capable
of theft," he said wearily, "but now, of course, you are
quite right. The rooms have been locked and will be
guarded until this matter of Miss Russell's death is re-
solved. Tell me. Will you be willing to complete the
inventory?"

"Surely," I said, "that will be a matter for the executor
to decide, and I have my own affairs to see to in London.
I will not be able to wait here indefinitely."

"Under the circumstances—" the inspector said, "and
you must forgive me if I continue to remind you that there
are 'circumstances'—I think that I will take it on myself to
direct that such an inventory be completed. You are, I
take it, well qualified to do the work. From what I have
heard of Lady Stewart, she did not tolerate incompetence.
And there is, I'm afraid, no possibility of your being allowed to return to London immediately. You understand
that, of course."

"All of us will have to stay here?"

He nodded his head slowly. His dark hair was thin-
ning at the temples, and there were gray pouches under
his eyes. I thought that I had never seen such an emaciated,
tired face. "Even Dr. Kubler, who seems to be particularly
anxious to leave," he said.

"We stay because we are suspects?"

"Yes." He broke into a fit of coughing which wracked his thin body. "All suspects. And now, if you please, Miss Haverlock, we will speak of motives and of opportunity."

"And means?" I added in a low voice.

"The means are known to us," he said. "Perhaps you may have noticed in the course of your work the gold cross which sat on a pedestal in a corner of the room where Miss Russell was killed?"

"Yes," I said. "It's a beautiful piece—sixteenth century. I think she must have found it in the Tagus area."

"I'm sure that you are right," the inspector said wearily. "To me it is simply a good cross—small enough to hold in one's hand, heavy enough to kill."

An hour before, when I had been outside and a peacock had screamed, I had visualized Marian's mouth open in a cry of terror. Now I saw more. A faceless form. The cross descending. The battered head. My hands grew icy cold, and the cigarette smoke seemed to choke me.

"You do not like to think of what happened," the inspector said. "Well, that is natural enough. Even the murderer did not care to see her face when she died. She was struck from behind—one blow only. It was enough. Tell me, Miss Haverlock. I am informed that you were working in the wing today."

"In the chapel," I said, finding as I spoke that my lips were numb. "Four rooms away."

"Away from what?"

"From—from the room where she was murdered."

For the first time there was some animation in that thin face.

"What makes you think that the murder was done there, in the room where she was found?"

"I simply assumed——"

"One can assume nothing. The cross was found there, true—matted with her blood and hair at its tip—and the body was found there as well. But that tells us nothing about where she was killed." He lit another cigarette. "You found the body?"

"Yes."

"It's position?" The weariness was gone from his voice now. The boredom he had conveyed was replaced by an intent eagerness.

"Wedged behind a suit of armor."

"Yes. I have seen it. There are traces of blood there, too. It must have been a shock."

His voice was sly now, insinuating.

"I thought she was alive," I whispered. "Her eyes were open."

"Alive? A curious impression, Miss Haverlock. Was she the sort of woman you would have expected to find in such an unusual place?"

"I thought that she was hiding," I protested. "I know it's absurd, but it never occurred to me that she might be dead."

"Hiding? And why should she be hiding?"

"I don't know," I told him. "That was my first impression. It lasted only a second. I shouldn't have mentioned it."

"You should mention everything," he told me. "Come. Think, Miss Haverlock. You may not consciously have thought of a reason that she might be hiding, but subconsciously——"

"Her fiancé had been looking for her," I said quickly.

"Ah! And is there any reason why she should have been hiding from Mr. Caravels?"

"Of course not," I said impatiently. "You're making something out of nothing. The last words that he said to me were about his having been looking for her, and naturally when I saw her——"

"Naturally?"

"Considering the fact that Mr. Caravels had apparently just walked past her without her calling attention to herself."

"It is somewhat difficult for a dead woman to 'call attention to herself,' as you put it, Miss Haverlock."

A thin smile etched itself on his lips.

"You can't possibly be making a joke out of this!" I said.

"No. There is no joke. I went too far, perhaps, but I was attempting to demonstrate that one may know—or intuit—more than they think. Perhaps this will be more meaningful to you later. For the moment you have been forced to remember more than perhaps you might have done about the events of this afternoon. You were many rooms away from the room where the body was found, you say."

"In the chapel." I did not know how to react to this man. His air of ennui had returned, but a moment ago I had been so tense that I could scarcely talk to him. Then he had confused me, made me angry. And now, surprisingly, I found that I could relax. I leaned back in the chair.

"You had been there all day?"

"No. Dr. Kubler will tell you that I talked with him for a few minutes in the morning upstairs."

"Where upstairs?"

"Outside Lady Stewart's room."

"And why had you interrupted your work to go there?"

"I wanted to see Lady Stewart to tell her that I had not been able to locate five items on the list she had given me."

"She had given you a list of her possessions?"

"No, only of about a hundred of them."

"She had asked you to check those particular items?"

"Yes."

"And may I ask why?"

"I think that she was afraid that some of her things might be missing."

"And it appears that she was correct. That is very interesting, Miss Haverlock. You went to tell her this?"

"Yes, but she was unconscious."

"And so you talked to the doctor instead. He is, I think, a psychiatrist?"

Despite the inspector's laconic air, the questions were coming fast, and each question was carefully chosen. I felt a sense of rising admiration.

"He is also a medical doctor," I said.

"You have proof of this?"

"It is what he told me."

"I see. And when you discovered that Lady Stewart was unconscious, did you tell him why you had come to see her?"

"No, certainly not."

"Why not? Did you think that Dr. Kubler might have been party to the thefts?"

"No. That had nothing to do with it. The conditions under which Lady Stewart had given me the list—well, I knew that this was a private matter."

I realized, too late, that he had made me say more than I had meant to say. No, that was not it exactly, but he had twisted things ever so slightly.

"What were these 'conditions' under which she gave you the list?"

I took a deep breath. There was no telling with this odd little man where my answers would lead me. "She called me to her room last night," I said, "at midnight."

"Awakened you at midnight?"

"I didn't say that. As it happens, I was outside the house until that time. When I came back, MacGregor was waiting for me with her message."

"And what were you doing outside alone? I would not think that a young woman such as you, a stranger to this place——"

"I was with David Ashor," I said. "We had taken a walk."

The inspector stared at me through a veil of smoke. "You are a good friend of Mr. Ashor's?"

"No." Now it was my turn to let exhaustion creep into my voice. "I met him for the first time when I came here."

"But it is perfectly natural that you should become friends quickly," the inspector said. "He is a handsome young man, and you . . . but I expect that is beside the point."

"I think that it is," I said stiffly.

For the second time he smiled that thin smile. "You will pardon me, Miss Haverlock," he said, "but you can see that one thing leads to another. But you have made your point. Lady Stewart wanted to speak to you in private—although, I take it, she was not usually surrounded with people."

"Senhora was always with her," I said, and I realized once again that I had said more than I meant to say.

"So Lady Stewart did not want even her companion to know that she suspected that certain of her possessions had disappeared?"

"It doesn't necessarily follow that she thought that Senhora might have been stealing from her," I said tartly.

"Many things do not necessarily follow," the inspector said, pulling a handkerchief out of his pocket and rubbing it across his bony forehead. "Only a few more questions, Miss Haverlock. To return to Mr. Caravels. After you returned from talking to Dr. Kubler . . . what time would that be, do you think?"

"I don't know. Perhaps eleven-thirty. It was before lunch at any rate."

"Yes. And Miss Russell was alive at luncheon. Did you have occasion to speak to her during that meal?"

"I ate in the chapel," I said. "A maid brought me my lunch."

"At your request?"

"No. Senhora had ordered it. She knew—they all knew —that I did not want to be interrupted."

"And she was eager that you finish the inventory as soon as possible?"

"I don't know," I told him. "The first time that I talked with Lady Stewart about the matter, Senhora was in the room, and she gave some indication that she was opposed to the inventory being made."

The inspector started to light another cigarette and then, sighing, returned it to the package. "And so you were in the chapel from eleven-thirty until the body was found—until you found the body, I should say."

"Yes."

"And the doors were open between the adjoining rooms?"

"They were."

"Did anyone interrupt you there?"

"Only the maid when she came to bring my lunch at about one."

"And Mr. Caravels. We must not forget Mr. Caravels. What time would you say he came?"

"I don't know. It was during the storm. We couldn't have talked for more than ten minutes, and directly after he left, I went to turn on the lights in the other rooms and found—found the body."

"I see." The inspector tapped his fingers against the top of the desk, staring at them as though they were moving without his consent. Then, with an impatient movement, he took another cigarette out of the crumpled package and lit it. "And Mr. Caravels came to see if you had seen his fiancée?"

"No," I said in a low voice. "He only mentioned that when he was leaving. He said that he had been outside in the courtyard when the rain had started, and that he thought that he saw that one of the windows in the wing was open."

The inspector stared at me over the flame of his match, letting it burn until it scorched his fingers. "But," he said, "those windows are set in grilled stonework. They do not open."

"I know," I whispered.

"Very well, then." The inspector pushed back his chair. "You have been most helpful, Miss Haverlock. I will not forget that you have been most helpful. There is only one further thing."

I rose, my hands clenched in front of me, tension pouring back into my body.

"I would not be as open with the others as you have been with me. You may feel that you know little that is of importance, but to the murderer small things may seem of the utmost importance. And it has always been my opinion that one murder is more than enough."

Instead of a formal dinner, a buffet was served in the dining room at nine. When I left the inspector, it was being set out, apparently under Senhora's supervision, together with the housekeeper, for I saw them both standing by the massive oak sideboard that lined one side of the dining room as I passed its open door. For the first time since I had met her, Senhora was not wearing the wrinkled tweed skirt and stretched-out cardigan but was dressed instead in black. I saw her face, drawn and haggard, as I paused in the hall, and for a moment her dark eyes met mine, and I saw the familiar flare of hostility in them before I hurried up the broad stairway to my room.

I lay for a long time in a hot bath, trying not to think, aware that my emotional exhaustion would allow no high degree of rationality to my thoughts. I would, I determined, live the time that was left for me at Alcombra on a day-to-day basis, completing the inventory as quickly as possible and keeping my own counsel, as the inspector had advised. Whatever else I did, I would not play guessing games with myself or anyone else about the identity of Marian's murderer. It would be enough for the inspector to point the finger of guilt, and from what I had seen of him, I thought that it would not be too long before he did so. I loathed the thought that anyone in this house could have committed an act of violence, but I believed that one of us had. And I wished that it would soon be over.

When I came down to the dining room, dressed in the most subdued article of clothing I had brought with me, a pale-gray cocktail dress cut in simple lines, I found only Claire there before me. She intended to make no pretense of being in mourning, if the red-velvet pants suit she was wearing was any sign. Her blond hair was high on her head in a mass of curls, and what appeared to be diamond earrings dangled about her face. She smiled over her shoulder at me as I came into the room and continued to heap her plate with food.

"I don't see why we have to wait," she said in the husky voice she usually assumed only with men. "I suppose it's dreadful of me to say it, but I'm famished. Make sure you have some of these prawns—they're absolutely delicious—and this dressed crab. *Santola recheada*, I think they call it. Ummm." She dipped a spoon in a casserole dish and closed her eyes as she tasted. "I don't know what this is," she said, "but it's simply marvelous. Whatever else you have to say about this place, the food is first rate."

I suppose that until that moment I had thought of her as simply a beautiful, rather silly woman who was accustomed to having her own way. But now, as she helped herself greedily to some sort of aspic, I found myself appalled by the extent of her self-absorption. It was not that I would have thought any more of her if she had made a pretense of caring that either Marian or her mother-in-law was dead. If she had worn black and come to dinner tearful and pretending to a lack of appetite, I would have been equally repelled. But she could have struck some middle course.

There were several decanters of wine on the sideboard, and while she took her plate to the table, I poured myself a glass of rosé. "There is a great deal about this house that wants changing, you know," Claire said, taking a seat at the head of the long table. "I shall have to get the decorators in as soon as it's possible. I don't expect Jerez would like to take on the job, but then one never knows."

I tried to keep my face expressionless, but she must have seen that she had surprised me. She laughed, delightedly. "Pour me a glass of Chablis, will you?" she said. "Why shouldn't I have the house redecorated if William and I are going to spend part of every year here?"

"No reason at all," I said, pouring her wine and taking it to her. It occurred to me that she was probably the sort of woman who finds it impossible to establish any sort of relationship with anyone unless she could somehow put them in the position of waiting on her in some way. It would, I determined, take more than this for her to arrive at any state of intimacy with me. Necessity dictated that for a while we would have to live in the same house, but I would make it quite clear, if I had to, that I intended to be neither her servant nor her confidant.

"I expect you're surprised that I should be making plans about the house," she said, patting her full mouth with her napkin and plunging her fork into the aspic on her plate.

"Why should I be?" I said crisply. I had thought a few minutes ago that I was hungry. After all, the last meal that I had eaten had been eight hours ago. But now, looking at her heaped plate, I found that my appetite had disappeared.

"Don't be so up-tight," Claire advised me. "You're really quite attractive, you know—or would be if you'd let yourself go. A woman should have a certain amount of—well, vitality. William always says——"

"Does he?"

With her mouth full, she looked up at me with slowly

narrowing eyes, and I knew that I had made myself quite clear, and that there was no longer any question of our being "girls together," if that was what she had had in mind.

"Everyone thinks that Alcombra is going to be turned into a museum," she said in a hard voice, "but that simply isn't true. The old woman had no right to make that sort of plan. The fact that she did is proof enough that she had totally lost her grip on reality."

That last phrase did not sound like her. I wondered whom she was quoting.

"She didn't have a thing when she married William's father," Claire said triumphantly. "Not a shilling, except some paintings her father had left her. William's father never cared anything about this absurd collection of hers except that it kept her out of his way. William told me that."

I expected that William had told her a good many things in whatever ratio of truth and falsehood was necessary to convince her to marry him. I wondered if he was sorry now that he had been so successful.

"And so," she continued blandly, "William deserves to have Alcombra. It's what his father would have wanted. As soon as these silly legal technicalities are out of the way——"

"Claire!" I looked to the door and saw William Stewart standing there. Ordinarily I saw him as only a stock figure—a fat, pompous man with a too-young wife—an ineffectual, bombastic middle-aged man who, I suspected, knew his own weaknesses only too well. But there was something in his face as he came into the room, his eyes pinned on his wife, that made me think there might be more to him than I had imagined. And Claire's reaction seemed to substantiate that. She seemed to shrink a bit, and the smile that she assumed was conciliatory.

"I was just telling Miss Haverlock that the crab is delicious," she said, rising. "Let me get you some, darling.

Here, sit down beside me and tell me what you'll have. There's some marvelous salad and. . . ."

He let her run on as she began to scoop bits of this and that into a plate, her back to him. But his eyes never left her, and there was a brooding expression in them, a pensiveness that I did not associate with the man. Then, suddenly, as she set the plate in front of him, he seemed to switch off whatever his thoughts had been.

"Soria's gone," he said heavily, addressing himself to me. "I expect he talked to you."

I nodded.

"He's a good man," William Stewart said, unfolding his napkin and placing it carefully over his stomach. "I expect he'll get this thing settled without too much delay. He's not leaving anything to chance, I can tell you. Two of his men are staying here the night."

"Why on earth would he do that?" Claire said lightly. "He doesn't think there'll be another murder, does he?"

Her husband ignored her. Taking one look at his plate, he pushed it aside. "David was looking for you a while back," he said to me. "He's down talking to Teles now— about the vintage. It's due to come off any day now, and we can't have it held up because of what's happened here."

"Who on earth is Teles?" Claire said with demanding playfulness, biting into a roll.

"He's the estate agent," her husband said. "I've told you that before, Claire. Don't you ever listen to anything I say?"

I took it from the triumph in her voice that her husband had a stance with which she was familiar, and that she knew she could deal with him now. But she had not been so sure of herself a few minutes before, and I knew that for some reason I would remember that.

"Teles is a good man," William Stewart said heavily, stabbing a bit of crab meat with his fork. "My step-mother never liked him. My father hired him to manage the vineyards before he died, you see. She had nothing to say about it. I don't know how many times since, I've heard her threaten to let the man go, but she never dared. Teles knows how to make those vineyards work, you see, and she needed the money to complete that collection of hers. Besides, she never liked to think about the farming aspects of this place. You see the way she cut it off from the rest of the estate with that stand of pines and the shrubbery. Not that when the vintage comes there's any way of forgetting what's going on down there. You can even smell the fermentation in every room of the house." He lifted the fork tentatively to his mouth and then put it down, the food untouched. "Not that she didn't try: windows closed tight, no matter what the weather. You've got to say this for her, she was a damn strong-minded woman."

I think that when he said that, I really realized for the first time that Lady Stewart was dead. I had known it before, of course. I had seen her body. But I had not, until that moment, had the sense that she was really gone. I think that was why he was reminiscing—to help to convince himself that only her memory lingered on in the house.

Jerez joined us then, taking a place beside me at the farther end of the table from William and his wife. He did not help himself to any of the buffet but sat, silent, his face ashen, steadily drinking glass after glass of port, which he poured from the decanter he had brought to the table. The silence was oppressive. William ate balefully, his eyes fixed on the wall. Even Claire had nothing to say until Martin Kubler came into the room, and then there was a little flurry while she advised endlessly on his choice of food and insisted that he sit beside her.

"The thing is," Jerez said to me suddenly in a low voice, "I can't understand why anyone would have wanted to kill Marian." He spoke as though we had been in the middle of a conversation. At the other end of the table Claire chatted vivaciously to Martin about her impressions

of the inspector, caricaturing him in a shrill voice, while
the doctor obviously did his best to change the subject. I
realized suddenly that as far as the others were concerned,
Marian might never have existed. Even David, when he
had talked to me in his room, had spoken only about the
way in which her death might affect us, not of the woman
herself.

"She didn't have any enemies," Jerez continued. His
dark eyes seemed to be imploring me to believe him. "Not
here, not anywhere. No one is going to benefit from her
death. I've been trying to reason it out. All afternoon I've
been trying to reason it out, but it doesn't make sense."

His voice broke, and he drained his glass. I found
myself wishing that David were here to help me with this
man, because he obviously needed help. David would
have known what to say to him, but I had always been
worse than useless in the face of the strong emotions of
others.

"I want to tell you that I'm more sorry than I can say
that I had that—that first reaction," Jerez said. "Accusing
you of being responsible. I didn't mean it, of course. It was
simply the shock."

"I know," I said. "It's all right." I could scarcely remember what he had said. That afternoon seemed so
very far away.

"I was extraordinarily fond of her, you know," Jerez
went on under the cover of Claire's laughter. "My God,
hasn't that woman any feelings?"

He glared at Claire, but her attentions were focused on
Martin Kubler, who had evidently managed to divert her
from the subject of the police. I heard her say something
about the wine going to her head. Her husband seemed
to have forgotten to eat and was still staring straight in
front of him.

"Perhaps she's nervous," I suggested with a generosity
I did not feel. "People act in strange ways when there's
been a—a tragedy."

THE WHITE PEACOCK 151

"You feel it, too, then." Jerez put one hand over mine. "I know you hadn't known Marian long, but you did sense, didn't you, that she was a very unusual woman?" I had felt no such thing, but it was impossible to say so.

"The only thing that I can think of," Jerez said rapidly, "was that whoever killed her thought that she was someone else. I mean, it was dark in that room. The murderer could have made a mistake."

"They would have known she was a woman," I said, startled. "And besides Claire and myself——"

"Someone could want her out of the way, couldn't they?" Jerez asked in a loud voice, glancing at the other end of the table. "She's a silly, malicious, self-centered woman."

He spoke at a moment when Claire had stopped talking. His words seemed to echo off the walls. Even William was startled into awareness. There was a long moment of awkward silence.

"I don't suppose you'd like to have a hand of cards, Kubler," William said. "Gin—or cribbage. There's a board about here somewhere."

"I think that I'll go to bed," Martin Kubler said, rising. "It's been a difficult day for all of us."

I left the dining room with him, eager to escape and yet hating myself for not having been able to say something to have mitigated the agony Jerez was going through —if it was agony and not simply a clever act. He had said that no one had had any reason to kill Marian, and I was willing to admit that as far as I knew, she had not constituted a threat to anyone in the household—except, perhaps, in some way I did not understand, to him. She had had no ties with William or with Claire. Martin Kubler was a stranger to her. Even her own son did not know her. She had been close to only Jerez. If anyone had had a reason. . . .

Martin Kubler was silent as we climbed the stairs together, but when we reached the top, he touched my arm. "I wanted to say one thing to you," he said. "It's about Senhora. From something that she let slip when we were seeing to—to Lady Stewart's things, I think that you should avoid her as much as you can. Probably this sounds overly dramatic, Miss Haverlock, but she's a vindictive woman, and in my experience vindictive women can be dangerous."

I think I knew the moment I stepped into my bedroom that someone had been there while I was at dinner. There was no overt sign of this. Nothing had apparently been moved. My cosmetics were still arranged as I had left them on the bureau, and when I opened the drawers slowly, one after another, my underwear and handkerchiefs were still in neat piles. Nothing seemed to have been disarranged in the closet. Even my notebook was still on the bedside table where I had left it. It was only when I looked inside it that I realized that the sheet of notepaper on which Lady Stewart had listed part of her possessions was gone.

I looked everywhere for it—in my purse, in the pockets of the slacks I had been wearing that afternoon, even on the shelves of the drug cabinet in the bathroom— though I remembered quite clearly having placed it, folded as she had given it to me, in the notebook just before I had come upstairs this morning to tell her about the missing items. When I had talked to Martin Kubler outside her room, the notebook had remained in my hand. And later, when I had been working in the chapel, I had tucked her list in the pocket at the back of the notebook so that the list would not slip out.

I sat on the side of the bed and tried to remember if I had kept the notebook in my hand when I had gone to turn on the lights in the five rooms. I thought that I had. I had certainly had it when I had gone with David to his room. I remembered placing it on the table beside my chair. And when William Stewart had interrupted us, had I brought it away with me? Obviously I must have done so, because it was here on the table beside my bed. There was the possibility that I could have left it in David's room, of course, and that after I had left, he had found it and brought it here. If that was so, he could have found the list and taken it. Was it simply because I did not want to believe such a thing that I imagined that I could recall placing it here myself?

There was no lock on my door. Anyone could have come in and taken anything while I had either been walking in the vineyard or been at dinner, or it was conceivable that despite the fact that I had tucked the list in the pocket, it could have fallen out. Whatever the answer, it was gone. And the realization made me tense with frustration. I needed that list. Obviously it was important, and although I could easily remember the five items I had not been able to locate, the list was my only proof that anything had been removed from the collection. From the interest the inspector had shown in what I had told him, it was more than possible that the fact that certain things were missing from the wing might be vital to his case—might, in fact, provide a motive for Marian's murder. Without the list, how could it ever be proved that anything was missing? Even with it, someone could always argue that Lady Stewart's memory had played her false. Perhaps, among her things, one could find bills of sale for what she had purchased over the past years. But even then there could be no certainty that some things had not been resold. No, her written word that certain items had been in her possession, or should have been, was the best proof of theft which could be provided. And whoever had taken it must have considered it incriminating evidence against him.

I felt a pricking of resentment. The inspector should have realized the importance of the list. He should have asked for it—taken it from me—but he had not even ex-

pressed a desire to see it. He had taken my word, and that
seemed strange. He had not impressed me as a man who
was overly impressed by people's words. Now I would
have to tell him that it was missing, and I did not relish
the thought. Apparently he had trusted me to keep it safe,
just as Lady Stewart had trusted me. I had failed both
of them—and myself.

And then there was another consideration. As far as I
knew, no one but myself and Lady Stewart and now the
inspector knew about the existence of the list. On those
grounds alone, he might jump to the conclusion that I had
destroyed it myself, for reasons of my own—incriminating
reasons. There was no way I could convince him that
anyone else could have known. I could not even convince myself. It was possible, of course, that MacGregor,
watching outside Lady Stewart's door that night, had
taken the occasion to listen to what she had been saying
to me. He might have subsequently told Senhora. I only
guessed that there was some antagonism between them.
Or perhaps Senhora had not told the truth about not having gone into Lady Stewart's bedroom after I had left.
I had found that odd to begin with. Perhaps Senhora had
gone to her and demanded why I had been sent for at
that time of night, and perhaps, weak and ill, the old
woman had told her. Perhaps that had brought on the
stroke, and Senhora, frightened at what she had done,
had gone back to her room and pretended subsequently
not to have discovered Lady Stewart's condition until the
next morning.

And then there was David. When I had gone with him
to his room, he had appeared curious about why his
great-aunt had wanted to see me. Perhaps he had had
some reason for suspecting the existence of the list. She
had been fond of him. They had talked together the day
before. She had told me herself that she trusted him—
and me. If she had told me about her suspicions, there
was no reason why she might not have told him. Perhaps

the list had not been drawn up then, but she had told him that she was going to make it out and give it to me. He could have come into this room as easily as anyone. He was supposed to be talking with the estate agent, but how could I be sure. . . .

I undressed slowly, my mind moving in diminishing circles. Only when I was in bed, with the lights off, did I come to the full realization that someone had actually been in this room, that some faceless person had gone through my belongings with prying fingers and eyes—or perhaps through only the notebook. But that was enough. Suddenly I was afraid. I discovered that I was lying stiff, every muscle tensed, gripping the sheets.

I forced myself to relax: took deep breaths, turned on my side, played all the tricks that I had played during those first long weeks of restless nights after Philip had left me. My thoughts had tormented me then, and they tormented me now as well, although in a different way. And now, added to the rest, there was that thin knife-edge of panic. I tried to think of something that would soothe me, and searching, I found only the dark corners of my mind. And then someone screamed. I sat bolt upright in bed, but it was minutes before I realized that it had been one of the peacocks.

Something or someone had disturbed them. I forced myself to get out of the high bed and went to a window. The moon was shining as brightly as it had shone the night before, when David and I had sat on the hillside. I could see the gray stone of the granite figure of the boar in the center of the courtyard. Even the white blossoms of the mimosa bushes were visible, speckling the darkness. And to the left of the courtyard, close to the cloistered walk that lined the wing, I saw the figure of a man.

For some reason, my first thought was that it was David. I had an unreasoning urge to throw open the window and call to him, but I waited, clutching the window-sill, and then he moved and began to cross the courtyard.

The moonlight fell full on him as he reached the figure of the pig, and I saw that it was one of the policemen Inspector Soria had brought with him. I could not see his face, but the cut of his uniform was unmistakable, and I remembered what William Stewart had said about two of the officers having been left behind.

I lit a cigarette then and paced the room in the darkness, trying to relax. But in that moment when I had thought that the man outside might be David, I had conceived a desire to see him, to talk to him. The night before on the hillside his presence had brought me a sort of peace. Perhaps if I could talk to him for only a few minutes, my nerves would uncoil.

Slipping on my black-silk wrap, I hurried out of the room, not giving myself time to think. He would surely be in his room by now. For some reason I knew that part of my tenseness was due to his having left the house. It would be something to know, simply, that he had returned. I turned the corner and saw the black-and-white-tiled floor of the hall stretch below me. I had forgotten the openness of the approach to his room. I knocked at his door and when no one answered, turned the knob, only to find the door locked. My first reaction was one of resentment. Why should he be able to lock his door when I could not lock mine? I turned and hurried back the way I had come, and as I did, I heard the sound of Claire's voice from below. Standing in the shadows of the bend in the corridor, I waited, listening, and heard William respond to her. There was no mistaking his voice, although I could not catch the words. And then I heard David speak—harshly, abruptly. My reaction was one of relief. He was back, then. That was really all I had to know: back safely. As I started toward my room, I heard Claire's voice again, and then Martin Kubler's.

They were all down there, then. Probably in the drawing room. Perhaps I should join them. Martin had said that he intended to go to bed, but obviously he had changed his mind. Or had he simply wanted to give me the impression that that was what he meant to do? Had they deliberately caucused without me? I laughed at my own paranoia—or tried to laugh. But the idea sparked a decision. I would not go down. I needed sleep, and I intended to get it. Closing my bedroom door firmly behind me, I went into the adjoining bathroom, took a sleeping pill, and climbed into the refuge of the high bed.

My mind was just beginning to unfocus when I heard a sound, and instantly I was wide awake. I opened my eyes and incredulous, saw the door swing open. A woman's figure was silhouetted against the dim light from the hall. Then, before I could speak, she was inside the room, and the door had clicked behind her. I lay motionless, hearing her heels click on the parquet floor. Where had I heard that sound before? Where. . . .

Then the light beside my bed flared on, and Senhora was standing not an arm's length away from where I lay. She saw me in the same instant that I saw her, and it was she who cried out. For a moment neither of us spoke. She was the first one to collect herself, smoothing her dark face into expressionless lines.

"I thought you were downstairs with the others," she said, her accent thickening her voice. "I came to turn down your bed. I'll leave at once."

She reached out for the light switch, but I caught her arm and at the same time pulled myself up against the pillows.

"Wait," I said. My heart was still pounding so hard that it was difficult to speak. "What did you really come here for?"

"I've told you," she said sullenly, pulling away from me and starting toward the door, a thin, straight-shouldered figure in black.

I was determined not to let her go without an explanation. I had always disliked and mistrusted her. How many times had she leveled accusations against me? Now it was my turn. Throwing back the covers, I slipped out of bed and ran across the floor, my tissue-thin nightgown tangled about my legs. I reached the door before her and pressed my back against it.

"I've been here two nights," I said, "and on neither of those nights has my bed been turned down. If it had been done, I would expect one of the maids to do it. Tell me why you came here. What did you expect to find?"

I expected some sort of sullen refusal, but instead she stopped where she was in the center of the room, her stiff figure duplicated by her reflection in the gilt-edged mirror.

"Proof," she hissed, her eyes glittering. "I expected to find proof!"

The venom in her voice struck me like a cold wind. I had realized when I had first met her that she hated me for what I represented—an interference in the pattern of life that had been established in the house—but I had never realized until now that she hated me for what I was. I remembered Martin Kubler's warning me that I should stay away from her, that she was a vindictive woman. But it was not my fault that she was here. She had come under her own volition, and now I wanted an explanation. I intended to have one.

"Proof of what?" I snapped.

"Proof that you're responsible for—for what's happened here." For the first time her eyes wavered from my face.

"A great deal has happened here," I told her. "What, precisely, do you mean? Do you think I murdered Marian Russell? Is that what you're saying?"

She shrugged her shoulders. "As if that mattered," she said scornfully.

"Then if you're not concerned with Miss Russell's death, you must be talking about Lady Stewart."

Her dark eyes seemed to slash at my face. "You killed her," she said. "She didn't have to die when she did. You killed her!"

"How?" I demanded furiously.

"You drove her to that stroke," Senhora cried. "When you went to her last night, you deliberately upset her. She was dead before you left her room. Why don't you admit it?"

I stared at her incredulously. "Because it's not true," I said. "She was perfectly well when I left her. You know that. You must have seen that she was all right when you went into the room yourself after I left."

The cords in Senhora's throat stood out as she tensed herself. "I did not go to her room until the next morning," she said shrilly. "If MacGregor told you that I did, he lies."

"Then there was a chance that he might have seen you."

"*Meu Deus!*" she hissed. "If you have told your lies to the inspector, you will live to regret it!"

"Just as Marian Russell lived to regret coming here?"

I was striking out wildly now, but she reacted. Throwing herself toward me, she tried to push me away from the door. Her nails tore at my arm. She was twenty years older than I, at least, but she had the strength of a peasant. Only by catching hold of the back of one of the walnut chairs did I manage to keep my balance.

"You said that you came here because you wanted proof," I said breathlessly. "Is that why you searched my room earlier? Is that why you stole the list?"

She seemed to freeze where she stood, her hand clutching the knob of the door. She turned her head toward me slowly, her eyes narrowing.

"What list?" she said in a low voice. "I know nothing about any list. Good night, Miss Haverlock. I advise you to say nothing of this to anyone."

It must have been a half hour after she had left me when, still pacing back and forth across the bedroom trying to regain my self-control, I found the list that Lady Stewart had given me tucked under a bottle of perfume on top of the massive oak bureau.

CHAPTER

7

The next morning the wind was high. It woke me with its shrieking, and from my windows I could see the pines bending under its force. My dreams had been full of the same sort of mindless fury, and I dressed quickly and hurried down to the kitchen, determined to spend the day engrossed in work. There would be no brooding over what had been done and said the day before. The events of yesterday had shaken me more than I cared to admit, and there was no escape from those memories except in total concentration on the inventory.

The talk in the kitchen was all of the wind and the storm that was approaching. The harvesting of the grapes had obviously taken precedence over murder and sudden death. For the first time since I had come to Alcombra I was aware that the farming of grapes was the major function of the estate, more important to the people who worked there than the personal tragedies of the inhabitants of the house. The word *roga* was repeated frequently, and the housekeeper explained to me, stiffly, that they were the men and women who served as additional pickers, called from the villages that dotted the mountains above the Douro. More of them would be needed if the grapes were to be harvested in time, and I took it, from what I overheard as I ate my eggs and freshly baked rolls, that David had gone to collect as many extra pickers as he could.

I had been afraid that I would meet Senhora in the kitchen, but she did not put in an appearance. As I crossed the broad expanse of the black-and-white-tiled hall, there was no sound in the house, or if there was, it was blotted out by the wailing of the wind. By the door that led to the wing I found one of the young policemen sitting listlessly in a straight-backed chair, his eyes shadowed with fatigue. It was necessary for me to explain who I was before he would unlock the door. Evidently the inspector had given him instructions to stay with me, for we made our way to the chapel together. As we passed through each of the five rooms, he carefully unlocked and then locked each door again. I realized with a sting of self-consciousness that the inspector did not trust even me to be alone here. It might be, of course, that he had ordered the officer to stay with me for my own protection. It was, I thought, more probable that the inspector entertained the suspicion I might be as capable of theft as anyone else in the household.

In the chapel, with the wind hammering at the stained-glass windows, I worked with absolute concentration for over an hour. The police officer did not speak, and when I entered the last item on my list, a sixteenth-century ivory relic portraying a figure that I thought I could identify as Saint Francis, I saw that the young man had fallen asleep, huddled in an old choir stall, with the carved face of a gargoyle leering at me through the shadows over his shoulder. I woke him reluctantly, realizing that he had been up guarding the house all night but always aware that if any charge of theft were ever brought against me, I did not want him to testify that he had not been watching. I had just touched his shoulder when I heard a key turn in the heavy arched door, and the inspector came into the chapel.

A cigarette was hanging out of the side of his mouth, but he bent and butted it out on the floor at once with a curiously guilty expression as though he was not certain whether or not the proprieties should be preserved, even though the room that he was in was no longer a place of worship but only an exhibit of sorts. The young officer pushed himself to his feet and stood at attention, staring at his superior with eyes still thick with sleep. The inspector muttered a few words of dismissal in Portuguese, and in a moment he and I were alone. I waited for him to say something, and when he did not, I expressed my appreciation that he had appointed someone to stay here with me while I worked, carefully keeping my voice free of irony.

He responded by shrugging his thin shoulders. His eyes were even more heavily shadowed than they had been the day before, and his thin face was like a gaunt mask. "I don't suppose," he said, "you've come across any of the missing items this morning."

I shook my head. "The few things that Lady Stewart designated as being in the chapel are here," I said, and then, remembering what had happened the night before: "Don't you think, Inspector, that you ought to have her original list? If it becomes necessary to prove that certain thefts have occurred——"

"Yes. Yes." His voice was impatient. "You're quite right, of course. Perhaps if you will make a duplicate list sometime today and give me the original——"

"I'd like you to have the original now," I said flatly,

taking it out of the pocket of my notebook and handing it to him. "You can provide me with a duplicate, or if you like, I will copy it in your presence. But I don't want the responsibility of keeping it any longer."

"Perhaps," he said, his fingers creasing the edges of the cigarette package that he had drawn involuntarily from his pocket, "you will tell me why you feel the sudden urge not to keep the list any longer, Miss Haverlock."

"It's a vital piece of evidence, isn't it?" I said sharply, certain that he was being purposefully obtuse. "At least it might very well be."

"It is your opinion, then, that Miss Russell's murder had something to do with the missing pieces?"

"I have no opinions," I said. Should I, I wondered, tell him that last night the list had been—for some short time, at least—taken from my room? Would that be fair? Because if I told him the entire story, it would carry with it the implication that Senhora had returned the list, and that, in turn, would imply that she had taken it. The question had nagged me last night until, with the help of another sleeping pill, I had fallen into a drugged sleep. Could I be absolutely certain that the list had not been there, tucked under the perfume bottle on the top of the bureau, all the time?

"All right." The inspector leaned against the wall, and it was as though his body caved in to meet it. "If you have no opinions, you may have convictions. A great many of your friends have these—er—convictions. Tell me, who do you believe killed Miss Russell?"

I stared at him, appalled, as the wind thundered against the glass above my head. I did not presume to understand this man, but I had never expected him to ask that question. "I have no idea," I said stiffly.

"Let me put it this way." He took a cigarette out of the crumpled package and smoothed it lovingly between his fingers. "Do you know of any reason that anyone here might have had to kill her?"

"No," I said positively.

"But you will agree that someone must have had a reason?"

"It may have been a mistake," I said, "an accident. There might have been a quarrel."

"And yet you heard no quarrel."

"People don't necessarily have to shout at one another."

"True. What you say is very interesting. Can you think of any other circumstance in which no motive would have been necessary—no long-term motive, that is? Assuming that it was manslaughter and not murder."

He was doing just what he had done with me before: making me draw hypotheses. I wanted to protest, but in a sense what he was presenting me with was an intellectual challenge, the sort of thing I had always found irresistible. It was a horrifying thought, somehow, to think that he could have so quickly taken my measure.

"She could have come upon someone in that room," I said quickly, "seen something she should not have seen."

"Another theft, perhaps?"

"Perhaps, or perhaps," I went on, unable to stop myself, half remembering another conversation, "the murderer mistook her for someone else."

He smiled thinly and giving up the struggle, lit the cigarette, immediately breaking into a spasm of coughing. "I see," he said when he could talk again, "that you have been giving this a good deal of thought, Miss Haverlock. And yet, as you say, you have no convictions in the matter."

"Have you?" I said boldly.

"A few, Miss Haverlock, a few. For example, I am convinced that she was killed near the spot where she was found. Her handkerchief, embroidered with her name, was found near the body, you see. Since you heard nothing, no sound of any quarrel, it might have been conceivable that she was killed elsewhere, and her body brought to that room to be hidden—to give the killer time."

"Time for what?"

He inhaled deeply. "Ah, about that, unfortunately, I am like you. I have no opinions, no convictions. That is why I had hoped that you might help me. You are the sort of person I find invaluable in such investigations, Miss Haverlock. You have an imagination, but a well-disciplined one—unlike others I might mention. Unlike Lady Stewart's companion, for example."

"Senhora?"

"That is what she is called, I believe. Her imagination is quite uncontrolled, and as a result, she has many answers—but not, I think, the right sort of answers."

He eyed me curiously, as though he had just made an important move in a game of chess and was waiting for me to make a predictable response. I thought that I knew the question that he wanted me to ask, and instinctive caution made me remain silent.

"Very well," he said, "if you will not ask me what I mean, I will tell you. The woman you call Senhora was waiting for me outside when I arrived a few minutes ago—in a rather agitated condition. She seemed to think that you would be telling me some tale or other about something that happened last night, and she wished to talk to me first, although as any woman should know, last words are often better than first."

"What did she tell you?" I said in a low voice.

He shrugged, grinding out the butt of the cigarette with his heel on the stone floor. "What do you think she told me, Miss Haverlock?"

"I don't like guessing games," I said briskly. There was a limit to the extent to which I could let this man manipulate me. "If you don't want to tell me, I'll start my work in the next room."

"She said," the little man purred, "that she had gone

to your room to turn down the bed and that you accused her of having come to steal something. At least that was the general tenor of what she told me. Is it true?"

"In a sense, yes," I said wearily, "but she was mistaken about my intention of going to you with the story."

"But why?" He mimicked disappointment. There was, I thought, something unpleasantly playful about his mood, despite his exhausted appearance. "Why should you not come to me with any story? You must know that I have a certain interest in what goes on in this house."

"Very well," I said. "Shortly before Senhora let herself into my room—she was under the impression, you understand, that I was downstairs with the others at the time—I had discovered that the list that Lady Stewart had given me was missing."

He stared at me in what seemed to be mock confusion. "How can that be, Miss Haverlock?" he said. "You have just given me that list."

"After Senhora left, I found it on the bureau," I said. "I decided not to mention the—the incident to you because I cannot be absolutely certain that it was not there all the time."

"But you do not think so." He was serious now, his eyes growing smaller in his thin face.

"What I think," I said crisply, "would not be admissible evidence in a court of law, and I find it difficult to understand how you could accept—"

I broke off as the little man raised one finger to his lips. Over the sound of the wind I heard someone's footsteps outside. They paused before the door, and then it slowly opened, and David appeared, his hair tousled, a streak of dirt smudging the right side of his face. It was obvious that he had not expected to find the inspector here.

"Ah, Mr. Ashor," Inspector Soria said happily. "To what do we owe the honor——"

"The storm is going to break in a few hours," David interrupted him. "I don't have time to talk. We've got to get as many people as we can into the vineyards to pick. I came to ask you if you'd help, Irene."

I stared at him, startled. He was tense, drawn to a fine edge of excitement. There was none of Martin's quiet confidence about him, but there was something that I found even more appealing, a sensitive response to the situation— an impulsiveness, the same impulsiveness that had made him shoot pebbles at my window that night. I remembered with sudden vividness the white of the moonlight on the hill, and I remembered the way he had opened himself to me. How curious that I had not realized until this moment that I loved him.

The inspector was saying something, but I did not hear the words. My eyes seemed to be caught to David's by invisible webs.

"Will you come and help, Irene?" he repeated in a low voice. "Will you come down to the vineyard with me?"

Again the inspector spoke, and I caught only the word "interview." Perhaps he was reminding us both that what he was doing was important, too. But questions and answers about death could wait. My life was what mattered now, and for the first time since I could remember I knew that I could do what I wanted to do rather than what I should do. Conscience was in retreat. What I wanted most to do was to be with David.

"Yes," I said eagerly.

The inspector rose. 'Before you run away with Miss Haverlock, Mr. Ashor, perhaps you might tell me how you were able to get in here. My officer had orders to lock each one of the rooms of the wing as he left us here and to stand guard outside."

"You kept the man up all night and failed to relieve him this morning," David said, taking my hand and leading me to the door. "It shouldn't come as any surprise to you that he's asleep on a chair in the hall. As far as the locked doors are concerned, I used my own keys. I have a key to every room in this house."

There was a silence. I knew the implication that the inspector would put on the admission. David would be suspect now, if he had not been before. But I did not suspect him. That was the important thing. Together we left the room, and neither of us looked back.

Five hours later the storm broke. There was no time to get back to the main house as the sky broke its hold on the rain, which descended in torrents, battering the vines and beating against the bent backs of the workmen carrying the last tall dark baskets full of grapes down the twisting yellow paths to the wine-press shed. I followed them, stumbling on the wet stone of the ladderways that jutted from the terrace walls, the rain dashing against my back. There were other women running, dark-faced peasant women, their black skirts swaddled about their thick bodies. Watching the men dump the loads of purple grapes, the women huddled under the eaves of the shed, their weather-beaten faces twisted in smiles as each man, ridding himself of his load, shouted "Io!"

Inside the shed a concertina played a melody that challenged the beating of the rain against the tin roof. The mood was one of gaiety because the grapes had been harvested in time. These people had been picking and carrying grapes from dawn till dusk for days. Clearly their lives had known little but back-breaking labor and poverty. The thin, unshaven faces of the men told their own story as they stood talking together in rapid Portuguese, their frayed trousers and patched shirts clinging, rain-drenched, to their bodies. But they were exhilarated because the harvest was in.

"You can't stand out here," a man's voice said in English. "Come on. Let's get inside."

It was Jerez, his usually immaculate clothing mud-

spattered, the tightly cut trousers torn at the pocket, his
dark hair clinging flat to his high forehead. He and Martin
Kubler had, I knew, responded to David's request for
help, but I had not seen either of them since we had
come out to the vineyard that windblown morning. I
followed him through the crowd of workmen and through
a low door into the shed.

We found ourselves in a long, low-ceilinged room with
a plank floor and the unhidden tin of the roof above us.
At the far end of the shed were the vats where I knew
the grapes gathered earlier were fermenting. There was
the thick, acrid smell of fermentation in the air, an overpowering smell that made me catch my breath. In another corner a man was sitting on the floor, playing the
concertina I had heard outside. Around him a few bare-
footed men were dancing a native dance, probably as old
as the hills outside. It was incredible, I thought, that after
their arduous toil they could have any strength left for
dancing. Vitality seemed to exude from them as they
laughed and clapped their hands in time to the music.

It was not until my eyes became accustomed to the
shadows that I saw David talking with a broad-shouldered
man, better dressed than the others although in work
clothes. I guessed that he was Teles, the estate manager,
or as David had spoken of him as we had left the house,
the *caseiro*. Teles had apparently been shocked when
David had suggested soliciting help from the main house.
"And, of course," David had said grimly, "he was right
as far as Claire and William are concerned. They'd rather
let the entire crop be destroyed than dirty their hands."

Now he turned his head and saw Jerez and me standing
just inside the door, but there was no sign of greeting in
his eyes. Turning away, he continued his animated conversation with the *caseiro*.

"It's a good thing we didn't do this for thanks," Jerez
muttered. "Here, here's a bench. Sit down. You must
be exhausted. I don't know about you, but I find it diffi-

cult to make out that young man—and just as difficult to think of him as Marian's son."

I made no response, but I knew precisely what he meant. I leaned back against the board wall, beginning now to be uncomfortably aware of my aching body. Jerez was right. I had not done this for thanks, but David's attitude bewildered me. When we had first met on that lonely mountain road, he had been gay and confident. Then that night on the hillside, with the moonlight holding us in its embrace . . . but it was better not to think of that. Better to remember that he was a stranger to me, a man who was capable of hatred for a woman who had abandoned him, a man who soon after her brutal murder could warn me that we would have to think of ourselves first. A man who had ignored me since he had tried to question me in his room. A man who, whatever else I might feel about him, I found I no longer understood.

"He's acting as though he were owner of this estate," Jerez said laconically, looking down at his hands, which, like mine, were scarred and red from the vines. "I suppose he may be the executor. Have you heard anything about the terms of the will?"

I shook my heard wearily.

"I suppose," Jerez mused, "someone had to take over although from what I hear, Lady Stewart left this business up to Teles completely. I wonder how he feels about David making his presence felt."

I glanced at the two men. Teles was talking, bending forward so that his broad face was close to David's. He was not smiling, and he gave the impression of someone making firm pronouncements, but the concertina was playing so loudly that I could not hear. More of the workmen had crowded through the door, and the air was thick and damp with the press of drenched bodies. Suddenly I felt as though I were suffocating. I started to rise from the bench, but Jerez caught my arm.

"You aren't planning to go back to the house just now,

are you?" he said. I could scarcely hear him over the
sound of the music and the clapping of men's hands. At
any other time I might have found this scene colorful, but
I was exhausted, and my head was beginning to ache. If
David had given any sign of gratitude, I knew that I might
have felt differently. There was exhilaration in the air.
I could have shared it.

I realized that Jerez was still speaking, enunciating
carefully to make himself heard over the sound of the
concertina. ". . . drenched. We might as well wait until
the rain lets up a bit. Those dirt paths we'll have to climb
will be pure mud. As far as that goes, we shouldn't have
to walk back at all. I mean, it would be unreasonable of
David to expect us to, wouldn't it? After all, even if it
weren't for the rain, it means climbing back up those
terraces again. There must be a road that goes back to
the main house, and some sort of truck. I'll ask him about
it."

"No!" I felt suddenly that I would not under any circumstances be a party to begging David to find us trans-
portation. I started to push my way through a cluster of
peasant women toward the door. I had just reached it
when someone caught my arm. Thinking it was Jerez trying
to dissuade me, I tried to pull away. Then, turning, I found
that it was David. His blue eyes seemed to be sunk in his
narrow face, and he was not smiling.

"Where are you going?"

"Back to the main house," I said. "It's too crowded
here, and I'm tired."

"Look," he said impatiently, "there's no need for you to
walk. I don't even know if you could get back up the
paths with it raining like this. If it's too crowded for you
in here, there's Teles's office."

"I don't want any special favors," I snapped.

As soon as the words left my mouth, I was bewildered
as to why I should have spoken them. David frowned.

"What's wrong with you, Irene?" he said. "I'd take you

back now in Teles's truck, but I can't leave until we get some details straightened out."

"I thought he took care of this part of things single-handed," I said, "and has for years."

"'With Lelia dead, he wants some assurance that he won't have to take the blame if something goes wrong with the vintage," David said angrily. "Believe me, this isn't easy for me. I don't know a damn thing about wine-making, but somebody's got to give him the authorization he wants. And since William wouldn't consider coming down here among the riffraff, it has to be me. Now, are you going to wait for me in his office, or aren't you?"

I wanted to tell him that I was not, but I knew that the only thing I would prove by going was that I was capable of playing the fool. I let him lead me across the crowded room to a small office containing only a battered desk, a file cabinet from which the drawers lurched drunkenly, and two chairs. A cracked piece of linoleum covered the floor. Only when David had left me there did I realize that Jerez had followed us.

"Well, this is more comfortable, isn't it?" he said with an attempt at cheerfulness. "I hope you don't mind if I keep you company. I heard David say that there was a ride back to the house in a truck in the offing."

He sat down on one of the chairs, and I saw the fingers of his right hand automatically begin to crease his trousers, mud-spattered and wet as they were. He caught my eye on him and laughed. For a moment he was like the Jerez I had first met that sunlit morning in the courtyard.

"Old habits die hard," he said. "I'm sure you'll believe me when I tell you that I haven't done any manual labor for—oh—twenty years at least. And even then, helping my father hoe a few rows of potatoes was about the extent of it. He's a poor man, my father. A small farm south of Lisbon. Even as a boy I didn't fit in, as you can guess. When I got my first job in an interior decorator's shop in the city, my family treated me as though I'd had some sort of mental aberration. Now that I have my own business—well, I might as well be living in another world as far as they're concerned. In a sense, of course, I am. Oh, I send them money, but we rarely meet. I learned a long time ago to loathe the stench of poverty. You can smell it out there, can't you?"

He waved his hand in the direction of the room we had just left. With the door of the office closed, the sound of the concertina was muted, but some of the men had begun to sing, and I could hear the words clearly enough. It was a fado, the words strangely formal, the tune melancholy:

> My eyes are two tapers
> That give sad light to my face,
> Marked by martyrdoms
> Of *saudade* and sorrow.

"It's just a familiar song to them," Jerez said scornfully. "They don't even understand what their lives are. They'll take the pittance they're given when the vintage is over and go off happy enough. They don't have any concept of the profit that a farm like this makes."

"How could they have?" I snapped. He was rambling on just as he had done when I had first met him, and, as then, he irritated me. "Do you expect them to understand higher finance when most of them haven't been given the beginnings of an education? My father loved Portugal, but he used to say. . . ."

"Yes?"

"It doesn't matter." It would, I realized, be easier for me to speak of Philip to a stranger than of my father. A few words of his, repeated, would do very little to show the sort of man that he had been, and I prefered to present him whole or not at all.

"You're annoyed with me," Jerez said. "I can't say that

I blame you. It isn't any good trying to explain to someone who's never been poor what it's like. Did Marian ever
talk to you about that, about what it felt like for her to
have nothing, with her aunt sitting on a fortune?"

I sat down in the chair behind the desk and propped
my chin on my interlaced fingers. If there was anything I
did not want at the moment, it was to be forced to remember—to remember anything. There had been one
excellent result to having put in five hours of hard
physical exertion. During all the time I had struggled
with the vines, my mind had remained as nearly blank as
possible. It had been enough to have been forced to concentrate on the elusive grapes. There was something about
this man's directness, however, that made it difficult to
rebuff him, as I had discovered before. And who could
blame him for wanting to talk about the woman who had
so suddenly and violently vanished from his life? There
were, I guessed, few other people at Alcombra who were
willing to talk about her in the way one talks in order to
deliberately conjure up a sense of sustained reality. I remembered with a twinge of guilt how I had left him in the
company of Claire and William in the drawing room not
an hour after Marian's body had been found, without
having uttered one word of consolation.

"Yes," I said slowly. "She mentioned how difficult it
had been for her."

"In what context?" Jerez said eagerly. "Forgive me. I
don't mean to pry, but somehow it's important that I
know what she said and what she did and what other people said to her during those days just before she died.
She hadn't talked much to me, you see. There was a—a
misunderstanding, I wanted her to go back to Lisbon
with me, you see. I didn't think she should stay here—
unwanted, without even the chance to talk to her aunt.
Senhora made it quite clear, you know, that the old woman
considered us intruders. I'm a proud man. I've never
wanted to stay where I wasn't wanted. Somehow Marian—

she got it into her head that I meant to leave without her."

The words seemed to pour out of him, hammering at my ears as the rain hammered against the tin roof. Obviously he badly needed to talk about something. I suspected that this was no idle conversation, and yet I could not see precisely where he meant it to lead. Whatever else, although I was willing to let him talk to me about Marian, even to ask me questions, I did not want to hear about their personal difficulties. Hurriedly I thought back to what his question had been.

"She had come to my room," I told him, "the day after we arrived here. She was upset about David being at Alcombra, too, of course. She wanted to talk to him, but I don't think she dared. She told me that Lady Stewart had prejudiced him against her. I think she talked about her past life because she wanted me to understand why she had given him up."

Jerez frowned, but he was obviously more comfortable now that I had shown my willingness to talk about Marian with him. He was, I guessed, a man who was happiest talking. It was one of those touches of the female about him.

"I don't understand," he said. "She didn't mention having this conversation with you. I don't know why. She used to tell me everything, but she'd changed since she'd come to this damn place. It was as though she was—was struggling with something inside herself, and she couldn't share it with me. When I wanted her to go, she said she couldn't run away. That was when we began to quarrel."

I could see that it was going to take a good deal of effort on my part to turn the conversation away from whatever had happened between him and Marian. Surreptitiously I glanced at my watch. It was after five. Surely David would be leaving soon.

"She wanted me to talk to David first," I told him, "to see just how hostile he really was to her. I think she wanted me to lay the groundwork. I mean, I think she wanted me to explain to him that as far as she was concerned, she had had no choice except to give him up when he was a baby."

Jerez shook his head. "Poor Marian. She had a very difficult life, you know—not just as far as David was concerned. When she finally married—well—she wasn't at all happy. I think, although she never admitted it, that she wanted desperately to give herself some sort of financial security, to prove to her aunt that she didn't have to be as much an inferior as the old woman had always made her feel."

He paused, buffing his fingernails against the palm of his left hand. "Did you?" he asked.

"Did I what?"

"Did you talk to David?"

Suddenly, over the drumming of the rain on the tin roof, I heard the silence of the night when David and I had sat together on the hillside. How difficult it was now to remember precisely what had been said and left unsaid. Only the memory of the mood remained, and it was bitter to think that that could never be recaptured.

"Yes," I said in a low voice. "I—I mentioned that she wanted him to understand why she wanted to give him up."

"And I suppose he made it clear that he didn't want to talk to her," Jerez said in a hard voice. "It was unforgivable what he did to her, you know. That next morning I saw her just after she'd talked to him. She'd lost her head, I think. Marian always was too emotional. I think she'd said things that never ought to be said. Anyway, she was completely distraught. She told me that she wanted to die, and then, just a few hours later, she was dead, wasn't she? You may think I'm a fool, but I can't help but wonder if her own son didn't have something to do with it."

The drive back to Alcombra was a nightmare of mud-slicked roads and blinding rain. I sat between Jerez and David in the cab of the truck and clenched my teeth to keep from crying out as we slid from one side of the narrow road to another. Only when we reached the gravel road that led directly to the house was there any traction for the wheels, and only then did I breathe easily.

The two men did not speak to one another during the drive. David bent grimly over the wheel, trying to see through the rain that battered the windshield, and Jerez pressed stiffly against the door. Occasionally I felt his eyes on my face, and I knew that he was trying to decide what my response had been to what he had said about David. In the tiny office I had turned the conversation aside with a determination that had kept him from pursuing the subject of David's possible guilt. I had tried to dismiss the subject from my thoughts as well, but I knew already that it was going to gnaw at my mind during the long lonely hours of the night. I did not think David capable of murder. Despite the fact that he might have quarreled with his mother, I could not think of any possible reason why he might have wanted to harm her, even assuming that he would have done so. And yet. . . .

When we climbed out of the truck, the wind caught us at the back and propelled us toward the rain-shadowed house. Inside, with the thick oak door shut against the storm, we found the hall in semidarkness. Muttering something under his breath, David clicked the light switch, but the chandelier overhead remained sightless. I heard a shuffling sound behind me and turned to find MacGregor coming toward us.

"What's wrong with the lights?" David asked.

The old man's bent shoulders moved in a hint of a shrug. "It's the storm," he muttered.

David ran his hands through his drenched hair. Behind

him Jerez stood stiffly, his dark face expressionless. Somehow he gave the impression that he was waiting.

"Where's the inspector?" David said. "He's still around, isn't he?"

MacGregor shook his grizzled head. "He went back," he mumbled.

"Back where?"

"To the town."

"I'll call him, then," David said as though talking to himself. "He ought to know——"

"Telephone's out," MacGregor muttered, and turning, he shambled away from us.

"I'm glad you're back." It was William. He came down the long stairs, his thick face set in worried lines. "I was afraid you'd been marooned down there. Did MacGregor tell you we're cut off completely? I don't like it, you know. I tried to keep the inspector here, but he said he couldn't risk being cut off from his office. In case of trouble, I suppose—trouble from some other source. The thing is, he'd sent those two men of his back earlier, and two other officers were supposed to have come to replace them—but no sign. I suppose the road to town is a stream of mud by now. I'll never understand why my father allowed himself to be talked into buying this godforsaken place, and now Claire——"

"The harvest's in," David snapped. "In case you wondered."

"Fine, fine." Clearly William was trying to present himself to us in his usual hearty manner, but something rang false. He was worried about something, on edge. But why shouldn't he be? I asked myself. Why shouldn't all of us be on edge? The storm and the sense of isolation it had brought with it would not, I knew, improve the situation. I was suddenly aware of my total physical exhaustion. I would take a long hot bath and lie down. And think. Or try not to think. I started toward the stairs.

"It was you I was really waiting for, Miss Haverlock," William Stewart said. "I know you must be tired, but I'm worried about Claire. Perhaps if a woman could talk to her. I mean, she admires you. You could make her see reason."

Throwing his cousin a look of disgust, David passed him and ran up the stairs. Jerez held his ground, watching and listening with what appeared to be intense curiosity but, for once, not intervening. I imagined that I disliked William Stewart almost as much as David did, but I found that I could not be as rude to the man as he had been. In fact, in some strange way, although my back was aching and I felt as though dirt were ingrained in every pore in my body, I sensed that I should make up in some way for David's abruptness.

"What's wrong with her?" I said wearily.

"That's the thing," William said, his plump fingers roaming up and down the line of buttons that pulled his tweed jacket tight about his bulbous stomach. "I don't know. She was in her room when the storm started, and when I went up to see what she was doing, I heard her talking to someone. I thought perhaps it was Martin." For a moment his pale-blue eyes were shielded by his lids as though he did not want me to look too directly at him. "She often talks to him to pass the time, you know. He's been our friend in London for some time, ever since Claire went to him. . . . But that's neither here nor there, is it? She's been upset, of course, because of what's happened here. I know that to you she seems quite—quite cool, but actually she's very sensitive. I thought that she probably wanted to talk to Martin alone, and so I went away. But then I came upon him reading in the drawing room, and I realized that she must be with someone else." He cleared his throat nervously. "And that was odd, you see, because you and Jerez and David were down in the fields, and I couldn't think of anyone else. . . ."

He paused and made a wide helpless gesture with his plump hands. "I'm not putting this very well, am I? But you see, I'm worried about her. Because she's locked the door, and I can't hear anything. I mean, she might be napping, but I'd like to be certain that she's all right. I mean, under the circumstances——"

"Surely," I said, "someone must have a key to the room."

"MacGregor has them," William Stewart said with sudden violence. "I know he has, because my mother always did trust them to the old fool, but he claims he gave them to the inspector."

"Did you ask the inspector for them?"

He stared at the tiled floor. "I didn't want to involve him," he said. "She might simply be angry with me. She's done this sort of thing, locking doors. You know what women are." He looked past me at Jerez as though seeking confirmation. "And later, when I became really concerned, the inspector was gone."

"But what do you think I can do?" I asked him.

"Well, you're a woman," William said with the air of having answered my question. "Claire's never had many women friends. Even when she was modeling, she didn't ever seem to be close to any of the other girls. There was too much competition, you know. It's a difficult business, that. I made her give it up as soon as we were married. She's had a hard life in many ways. And now—well, sometimes she doesn't seem to be able to talk to me. Even those sessions with Martin . . . and he's a fine psychiatrist. It was Claire's idea that I bring him here." He rubbed one hand across his forehead. "I'm rambling," he said. "I always do that when I'm upset. Claire says. . . . You could at least knock on her door and see if you can get some sort of response." There was a sudden belligerence in his voice. "You could do that, couldn't you?"

Nothing that he had said had given me any reason to think that I would be more successful than he had been, but he was right. I could do what he asked. I could understand why he was worried. I only wished that I was not so incredibly weary. That the inspector were here. That the wind and rain would stop beating at the windows.

He followed me up the stairs, and so did Jerez, both of them hesitant, as though they were expecting me at any minute to tell them to leave me alone. But I didn't want them to go. Without lights the house assumed the same ominous quality that I had sensed in the wing. It was nearly dark in the upstairs corridor. Someone would have to bring candles soon, or lamps. William indicated a closed door with his outstretched arm and then stood a little distance away with Jerez beside him as I knocked.

There was no answer. At the end of the hall the long window rattled under the onslaught of the wind. Then there was a pause. A silence. I do not think that I had ever heard a silence so complete. I called her name, softly at first and then, in response to my rising concern, more loudly. When she answered, her voice was muffled as though something was pressed to her mouth.

"What do you want?" she said. I could scarcely make out the words. "Leave me alone."

At least she was alive. I had not realized until that moment that in the back of my mind had been the memory of Marian Russell's lifeless eyes as her body had slid from its hiding place behind the coat of armor. I glanced at William and saw his heavy body sag with relief. I pointed at the door, asking him without words if he wanted to take my place. He shook his head, and I saw him mouth the words "Ask her to let you in."

And so I asked, expecting refusal, but without warning, the door was flung open. She was wearing a crumpled pink nightgown that hung off one shoulder, disclosing most of one breast. Her hair was disheveled, her eyes red-rimmed —and riveted on me. If she was aware that anyone else was in the corridor with me, she gave no sign.

"Very well," she said in a hard voice that bore little

relationship to the childlike wispiness she usually assumed. "Come in if you want to. You're supposed to be clever, aren't you? Perhaps you can tell me what to do."

There was no way of refusal. After all, I had sought her out, not the reverse. What excuse did I have for having bothered her if I now refused to talk to her? It did not occur to me until the door closed behind me that I could have simply left her with her husband. But if what William had said was true, in all probability she would have slammed the door in his face.

"You're wet," Claire said accusingly, throwing herself down on the bed. "That's right. You went along to the vineyard, didn't you? I told David that I wouldn't think of playing peasant, even if it meant losing every grape."

She said it triumphantly, as though she had accomplished some coup. I did not answer. I had not come into this room for the purpose of admiring her strength of mind.

"You'll find a housecoat in the closet," Claire said. "You'd better change, or you'll catch cold."

I ignored the suggestion. If I were going to change my clothes, I would do so in my own room.

"Your husband is worried about you," I said. "He asked me to find out what's wrong."

She laughed scornfully. "That's like William," she said, "to send someone else to do the dirty work."

I had never disliked her more intensely. "He knocked on your door several times," I said, "and when you didn't answer, he was afraid that something had happened to you."

The bedroom was a near duplicate of mine, with the addition of a single easy chair. There were four long windows against which the rain pounded with monotonous steadiness. What light there was, was slate-gray. Every chair and table seemed to be covered with discarded clothing and cosmetics. In the shadows of the far corner I detected an open suitcase. I wondered if, for some reason, Claire was preparing to leave Alcombra in spite of the inspector's order that all of us should remain.

"What's wrong with the lights?" she said now, querulously.

"The storm has evidently knocked down a line," I said wearily. "Since you seem to be all right. . . ." I started toward the door.

"Don't go!" She propped herself erect. "I want to talk to you."

"About the lighting arrangements?" I said dryly.

"No. I'm sorry. I'm not behaving very well, but I've had a shock."

I waited, my back to her.

"You don't really care, do you?"

"No," I said, "not really. But if I can help you, I will."

"It's that woman," she murmured. "No. Look at me. I'm trying to tell you something important. I can't tell William—not now. He may have had something to do with it. Don't you understand how terrible it is not even to be able to trust your own husband?"

I turned and looked at her. She had pulled the pink nightgown up over her shoulders and was busy wrapping a quilt around herself. "It's so cold," she said. "Ever since she came, I've been so cold."

"I don't know who you're talking about," I said, trying to keep my voice even. I was cold, too. My clothes felt like a wet shroud.

"Senhora. Who do you expect? She had the nerve to come in here and accuse me of. . . ."

"Of what?"

Throwing off the quilt, Claire slipped off the bed and made her way across the shadowy room to a low table littered with clothing. As she passed me, I realized that she had been drinking. Her pink nightgown billowing about her slim body, she left behind her the odor of whiskey and expensive scent.

"Have you ever seen this before?" she asked.

She had taken something from the mess on the table and was holding it out to me. Whatever it was, it was too small for me to see through the dusk. I went to her and saw, cradled in the palm of her hand, a ring. Taking it from her, I saw the glitter of a dark stone—a ruby. The gold band was very thin, molded as it touched the stone into what appeared to be two dragon claws. I recognized it immediately from the description on the list Lady Stewart had given me. It was the ring that was missing from the collection.

"Well, have you ever seen it?" Claire asked shrilly.

I chose my words carefully. "Where did you find this?" I said.

"I asked you a question first," Claire said petulantly.

"No," I told her. "I've never seen it before." That, at least, was true. I wanted to hear what else she had to say before I volunteered any more information.

"That woman said that I'd stolen it," Claire muttered. "That's a lie. I told her it was a lie."

"Where was it found?" I repeated.

"She *said* she found it here," Claire said defiantly, "in the top drawer of that bureau."

I took a deep breath. "What was she doing looking in drawers?" I asked her, trying to keep my patience.

"That's what I wanted to know," Claire said angrily. "She may think she's mistress of this house now, but she had no right to go through my things. Of course, she had an excuse. She said that she was helping the maids, putting away some of my clothes. A likely excuse. She was prying. I told her straight out that I wasn't going to put up with it. I told her that William would see that she was sent on her way. That was when she accused me of having stolen this from the collection."

I folded my hand around the ring. She seemed to take no interest in having it returned, and it was just as well,

I thought, that I keep it. "How did it get in the drawer?" I said slowly.

"How should I know? I never set eyes on it before. Who'd want an old thing like that? That's not the sort of thing I care for, someone else's castoffs. If you ask me, I think she put it there herself—to try to make William and me look bad. She said she was going to take it to the inspector, you know. That was before I took it away from her. I thought I was going to have to knock her down. She knew I meant business. There are some things I won't put up with, and being called a thief is one of them." She was talking with random spitefulness, but all the time her blue eyes were clinging to me. "Why doesn't someone do something about the lights?" she asked plaintively.

I had one more question: "Why didn't you tell your husband about this instead of frightening him the way you've done?"

"I won't be told what I should or shouldn't do," she said, flaring up, and it took me a moment before I realized that it was me and not him that she was talking about. "Oh, all right," she went on, sullenly. "I didn't want to tell him because he'd make a fuss. He never thinks I handle things properly. I mean, that woman may have gone to him and told him God knows what lies about the way I treated her."

"Because you took the ring away from her?"

"I may have hurt her a bit," Claire muttered. "I don't know. She said she was bleeding."

I clenched my fingers so tightly together that the ring hurt my hand. "Bleeding?" I said. "But you said——"

"I tried to frighten her," Claire said, suddenly furious. "Do you blame me? She was trying to blackmail me, wasn't she? I was simply protecting myself. I had a letter knife, and I——"

"You stabbed her with a letter knife?" I said incredulously.

"No, I didn't stab her. I may have cut her arm a bit. I

don't know. She deserved it. I had to make her give me that ring. She was staying terrible things: that there was a lot else missing from the collection, and that she wouldn't be surprised if all the things were hidden in this room. That's what I've been doing: hunting for anything that shouldn't be here, turning out the drawers."

"But why not tell your husband?"

"Don't talk like a fool," Claire hissed. "Don't you understand? If she really did find that ring in the drawer, it wasn't me that hid it here. And if it wasn't me, it must have been William. He could have done it, you know—stolen things. He told me when we came here that he didn't intend to go back to London empty-handed."

CHAPTER

8

It was when I turned away from Claire to stare out the long window that I saw, through the gray threads of rain, a flickering light. Her room, like mine, looked over the courtyard, now lost in the thick shadows of approaching night. It took me a moment to realize that the light came from one of the windows of the long gallery in the wing where the collection was housed. I caught my breath as the red glow turned to orange, spreading like an opening hand. It was not a candle flame that I was looking at or the glow of a lamp, but fire—fire raging out of control.

I ran to the door, threw it open, and smelled the faint musky scent of smoke. Behind me I could hear Claire babbling something about my not leaving her. I ran down the corridor toward the balcony that overlooked the main hall, hearing my own voice, shrill and unfamiliar in my ears.

"Fire!"

As I reached the head of the stairs, David came out of
his room. The smell of smoke was more powerful. There
was no need for him to ask me any questions. Together
we ran down the slippery marble stairs into the dusk below. At the bottom he paused.

"The collection!" I gasped breathlessly.

I did not remember until much later that the door to
the wing should have been locked. David threw it open,
and over his shoulder I saw nothing but darkness. The
smoke was thick, stinging my eyes. By the time we reached
the second door and found it open, I could see, far ahead
of me, the flickering tongues of flame.

David shouted something at me, but I did not take in
the words. The house was stone on the outside, and I did
not think that even the tile of the roof would burn easily,
but the interior of the wing was paneled in old oak that
would burn like tinder. It might be pouring rain outside,
but in here it made no different. And someone had opened
the connecting doors. As I ran behind David through the
crowded rooms, I realized that someone had deliberately
wanted the fire to spread, that it must have been set.

But there was the chapel! As we reached it, my mind
seemed to work with a sudden clarity. The floor was stone
here. Even the walls were of stucco in an attempt to cre-
ate the original effect. Beyond, in the long gallery, I could
hear the flames crackling. The smoke made me gasp for
breath. If we could shut the gallery off, there might be a
chance. . . .

In the doorway David came to a stop, shielding his face
with his hands. Looking past him, I saw that the long
velvet drapes that lined the window farthest from us were
in flames. At the end of the room the painted face of Lady
Stewart as a girl stared blankly at us through the welling
smoke.

"Get back, Irene!" David shouted at me. "I told you to
go back! Get help!"

"Too long," I gasped, the smoke choking me. "It will take too long, even if the telephone were working." I grabbed his arm. "The walls haven't caught yet! We've got to try to put out the fire in the drapes."

For a moment he stared at me through the swirling smoke, and then, reaching past me, he slammed the heavy oak door behind us and ran toward the flames. I followed, coughing and gagging, knowing that I should cover my face with something but knowing, too, that if we were to do what must be done, we would need both hands free.

We started to tear at the drapes, I on one side of the long window, David on the other. Where it touched the floor, the thick velvet was not yet aflame. I sank to my knees, tugging, twisting, struggling with the heavy cloth, scarcely aware of the tongues of fire licking the air above me until I heard David shout my name. Looking up, I saw the great mass of blazing cloth descending. It was too late for me to get out of the way. Before I could throw myself to the side, a blanket of flames engulfed me, suffocating me in blazing heat, wrapping me in a fiery cocoon.

Then I was being torn out of the layers of flame, and David's body was heavy against mine as we rolled together across the floor. My eyes still closed, I felt him press his hands over my head, felt his long fingers in my hair, and knew that the fire must still be blazing there, although I could feel nothing but his hands and body.

"I'm all right," I gasped. I opened my eyes and saw nothing but his. We rolled apart. I forced myself to my knees and reached for his outstretched hands. Together we rose. Across the room the drapes were smoldering into ash on the parquet floor. I watched, unable to move, as David went to the window and wrenched it open. I saw him gather the blackened cloth in his arms and shove it out into the courtyard.

After that there was silence. David was standing by the window, looking out. The wind pressed his blond hair close to his narrow skull. I went to stand beside him,

letting the rain drench my burning skin as the storm swept
through the gaping glass-toothed window. It was dark now.
No lights showed from the windows opposite. I wondered
if Claire was standing where I had stood a short while
ago. Had she watched the flames being extinguished with
relief, or had she wanted the wing to be gutted? Was that
why she had not followed me, had not brought help?

I remembered the ring then. It had been in the palm of
my hand when I had stood talking to her in the bedroom. I
could not remember putting it down before I ran out of
the room. Could I, in my panic, simply have dropped it?
My heart seemed to stop. I had been frightened a few
minutes before. No, terrified. Until the last tongue of
flames had been extinguished, I had been terrified. But
this feeling of dread was as bad—worse. I groped in the
pocket of my slacks. It would have been natural if I
had automatically put it there. Thank God. I had.

David, a stranger with a smoke-blackened face, moved
away from the window to face me.

"Are you all right?" he asked.

I wanted to give him the simple answer he expected. I
knew that simply because we had come through this
together there was no reason for me to expect that we
would suddenly be as close as we had been that night
on the hillside. We *had* been close then—and gay. It
seemed a very long while ago.

"I'm fine," I said, choking on the words. Or was it the
smoke?

"You've burned yourself," David said in a low voice,
"on your forehead. Let me see."

His hands cradled my face, and suddenly he was no
longer looking above my eyes but into them. Then his
mouth was warm on mine. Only for a moment, but after
that I clung to him. Until I could breathe again. Until the
door at the end of the long gallery creaked open, and I
saw William Stewart coming toward us, a candle in one

hand, the other pressing a handkerchief over his nose and mouth.

"My God!" he sputtered. "This is terrible, isn't it? Really terrible. Claire just told me. I've directed the others to stay outside until I could find out how bad it was. You don't mean that the two of you——"

David released me. "It wasn't as bad as it looked," he said coolly. "The drapes were on fire, and the Sargent of Lelia is completely destroyed. But there isn't much other damage—unfortunately."

The candle made a hollow of light in William's face, stripping it of its plumpness. His eyes seemed to waver in the flickering glow. The wind bursting through the broken glass was dispersing the smoke rapidly. Hesitantly he lowered the handkerchief. Except for the pool of candlelight, we were in total darkness.

"I don't know why you say 'unfortunately,' " William protested. "This was a very brave thing for you and Miss Haverlock to do. When you think of what could have been destroyed. . . ."

"If it had been," David said, "there wouldn't have been any bother about trying to break Lelia's will, would there?"

"I don't know what you're trying to say," William said stiffly. "If you're implying that I have any reason to want these—these beautiful things destroyed, then you're quite mistaken. I may have thought that my stepmother put entirely too much time and money into collecting them, but I assure you that I know their value."

"I'm sure you do," David said. I stared at him curiously. Too much had happened in too short a time. I was not certain what was happening now or what he was trying to make happen.

"Well, then, I don't know what you meant by using the word 'unfortunate,' " William said stubbornly.

"Someone is going to think that it was most unfortunate that the fire was put out," David said with slow deliberation, "and that person is whoever set it in the first place."

"But surely you can't believe——"

"How else would it have started?" David asked. "Spontaneous combustion? I think you'll have a difficult time convincing our friend the inspector of that."

"Look here!" William exploded. "It's not my function to convince him of anything. The fact remains that I don't believe that this fire was set."

"Don't you?" Bending, David scooped up some of the charred remains of a drape and held it to his nose. Then, passing it to his cousin: "Don't tell me you can't smell what I can smell. This cloth has been drenched in oil."

He was right. Even at a distance I could smell it, a pungent, sour odor.

"You can't hold me responsible!" William said, waving the candle back in front of us excitedly. The wavering light caught, for a moment, the painted sneer of a seventeenth-century Portuguese nobleman. "I wasn't anywhere near this gallery. I can't imagine who would do such a thing."

"Perhaps the inspector can," David said grimly, taking the candle from the fat man and starting up the long hall toward the door. "I'm going to send a messenger into the town to inform him of what's happened. It wouldn't surprise me if he came trotting back here, pronto—storm or no storm. You can tell him where you were or were not when the fire started."

"And so can you!" William Stewart bellowed, and then, to me: "Come along, Miss Haverlock. It's obvious that he's quite capable of leaving us here without a light."

We followed David like obedient children, back through the chapel and the five crowded rooms, their contents lost in darkness. My legs were weak with exhaustion. I was too tired even to remember with clarity the moment David had held me in his arms. Whatever he had felt in that moment, he was obviously capable of ignoring me now. I loathed this grim determination into which he seemed so easily to slip. It was a pity that Alcombra had not burned to the ground. At least then all of this would be over, and we could go our separate ways—all of us. And forget.

What appeared to be the entire household was waiting for us in the grand hallway. They huddled together in the center of the black and white expanse, Jerez standing a little apart from the others, his eyes watchful. Someone had set out candles on the tables that dotted the sides of the huge room, and the flickering light threw shadows on the floor, a clustered set of shadows like stalagmites.

"Is the whole house going to burn down?" Claire asked shrilly. She was standing a little apart from the house-keeper and the gaggle of maids. "Because if it is, I want to have my things removed from my room immediately."

"The fire's out," David snapped, "but the inspector should be sent for immediately."

"I've sent the gardener's boy, sir," a creaking voice announced as MacGregor stepped out from behind the women, his old head jutting forward like a turtle's from his hunched back. "He'll see that the village fire department is alerted as well, although with the roads in the condition they are, I shouldn't think their trucks could get through."

It was the longest speech I had ever heard the old man make. Even in the dim light I could see that something about him had changed. He still tottered back and forth on his feet, as though it was an effort for him to remain alert. There was still the air of feebleness. But beyond that there was a certain excitement, as though, had he been able, he could not have prevented himself from breaking into a jig. He shuffled on toward David until he could look directly up into the younger man's face.

"You shouldn't have put the fire out, sir," he said, his voice heavy with the Scottish burr that I had noticed before. "There's something evil about those things. Satan's playthings, that's what I called them. Told her to her face they'd bring her nothing but God's wrath. 'Thou shalt not covet,' I told her, but she didn't listen. Not her."

"That's enough, MacGregor," William Stewart said stiffly. He was, I could see, priming himself to take command of the situation. His chest puffed like a pigeon's as he confronted the servants. "As my cousin has told you," he said, "the fire has been put out. There is nothing to be concerned about. All of you are quite accustomed to doing without electricity. That should present no problem. It is now eight o'clock." He peered at his watch as though it were important that he verify the fact. "We will expect dinner by nine. There will be six of us, won't there? Tell me, where is Dr. Kubler?"

"I'm here." The voice came from the darkness of the upper reaches of the stairs. Like a Greek chorus, we turned to look into the shadows. There was a long pause, a silence. Martin Kubler neither descended nor spoke again.

William Stewart cleared his throat. "I think, my dear," he said to his wife, "that you had better see about changing. The housekeeper or MacGregor here will provide you with a candle. Hurry along now."

His voice took on a sharp edge, and I realized that Claire had not bothered to throw on as much as a negligee over the pink nightgown she had been wearing when she and I had talked in her bedroom. The strap had slipped off her right shoulder, revealing the top of her breast, as it had done when I had first gone into her room, and now, with her husband's eyes on her, she pulled it up angrily and started toward the stairs, a wraithlike figure in the dusk.

"Wait," David said in a loud voice. "No, I mean all of you. Dinner can be a bit late if necessary. Until the inspector arrives, I want all of you gathered in the drawing room. Yes, everyone. You, too, MacGregor. And Martin."

He spoke up into the darkness, and slowly the tall figure of the doctor emerged into the reach of the candlelight. He moved toward us slowly, reluctantly, his face expressionless.

"I'll be only a moment," Claire said. "Look here. I need a light if I'm going to go upstairs."

"You're not going upstairs," David said.

"Well, then, one of the maids can go," William said, puffing. "I can't have my wife——"

"No one is going anywhere," David told him. The candlelight threw his eyes and forehead into pale relief. "All of us are going to remain together until the police arrive. There'll be no more fires, no more murders, no more violence—at least until the inspector takes over again."

"See here, David," William Stewart said heavily. "You have no responsibility for what goes on here. If anyone should take control of this situation, it should be me."

For a long moment David simply looked at him. I heard Claire laugh softly near the stairs. When I glanced at her, I saw that Martin Kubler had bent to say something to her. The smile vanished from her face.

"We'll wait in the drawing room," David said in a low, evenly paced voice. "When the inspector arrives, he can decide what ought to be done next. Until then everyone is to stay together."

As the housekeeper and the maids turned to cross the hall, MacGregor muttered something under his breath. He was still standing in front of David, dwarfed by the younger man's height. I could not catch everything that he said, but I heard the name Senhora, and suddenly I realized that she was not here with the others.

"Missing?" David said. "What do you mean, she's missing?"

The old man raised his head. His hooded eyes were lost in the shadows, but his sunken mouth was twisted in something like a smile. "Gone," he chortled. "Look for yourself if you don't believe me. She's nowhere in this house."

While the others trooped into the candle-lit drawing room, William wearing a belligerent expression and draping his jacket over his wife's bare shoulders, David talked to me alone.

"You don't have to do this, Irene," he said in a low voice, "but you're the only one I trust—even Kubler. I can't be sure about him because of his relationship to William. I don't want any of them roaming about this house, but I can ask you. . . ." He took a deep breath. He had picked up one of the candles in its silver holder, and the light flared upward over his drawn face. "I want you to go to Senhora's bedroom. You know where it is, don't you? Next to Lelia's."

I nodded.

"I only hope I'm not making a mistake," he said, "asking you to do this, but I believe MacGregor. He may know more than he's saying about where she is, but I believe him when he says she's not in this house. We've got to find out what's happened to her, where she's gone. We can't wait for Inspector Soria to turn up, and there may be some indication in her room, some indication of where she's gone. If she's taken her clothing, well, that will give us some hint. Will you do it?"

I did not relish going anywhere alone in this shadow-stricken house, but I understood him. I knew that we had to make some attempt to find her. I had sensed for some time that she was a desperate woman, although I did not know why. The fact that she had searched Clarie's room and subsequently confronted her with the ring meant something. There were so many puzzle pieces that did not seem to fit, but perhaps they had fitted for Senhora. Perhaps she had made some sense out of what had happened here. And if she had, she was in danger. The least I could do was to go to her room.

"No," David said before I could answer, "I haven't any right to ask you to walk around this house alone. Listen. You go into the drawing room with the others. Make them stay there."

"I can't do that," I murmured. "William's chafing at the bit. It's hard enough for him to take orders from you. He certainly won't take them from me. Give me the candle. I'll see what I can find in her room. I'll be all right. If Senhora isn't in this house, well, then there's no one here but them." I pointed at the door to the drawing room and tried to laugh. "I can't be hurt by ghosts."

For a long moment his eyes met mine. "All right," he said, "go on, but don't take more than ten minutes at the most. If you can't find anything in that time, well, at least we did what we could."

He stood in the hall watching me as I mounted the long stairway. At the top I turned and looked down at him, and then I hurried along the corridor, past Claire's bedroom, the door ajar. Past my own. The candle cast jagged fingers of light on the carpeted floor as I turned the corner, moving soundlessly. Past the marble statue behind which I had hidden the night William and Senhora had stood there talking. She had said that she would not help him prove that Lady Stewart was mad. Had she, I wondered, already suffered the penalty of that refusal? I tried to keep a tight rein on my imagination. Simply because one woman had died was no reason to think that Senhora had been harmed. For all I knew, she might have fled Alcombra because of her own guilt. In the end we were probably all capable of any enormity.

I twisted the knob of her door, not giving myself too much time to think, aware that my own panic was lurking just beside my consciousness, as nebulous and yet as

real as my shadow tottering on the wall behind me. The
door swung open, and I stepped inside. There was a
strange odor in the room—an acrid smell. A mirror hung
opposite me on the wall, a gilt-edged mirror high on the
wall. I could see my face. And then another. Another
face! I could not breathe, could not move. It was a
man. Dark, glittering eyes met mine in the glass. It was
the man David had been talking to in the wine-press
shed. The estate manager. Teles! In the glass he seemed
to loom over me, and I saw the reflection of the long, thin
knife in his hand.

I threw myself to the side, at the same time pressing
my hand over the flame of the candle. We were in darkness. And then the silence! Yet I knew that he was there
beside me. In a moment he would move. Or speak. Every
sense straining, I waited. Not breathing. Aware that in a
moment I must scream or die.

He moved at last. I heard his feet on the parquet floor.
Shuffling. I heard him shuffling toward me. I knew that
at any moment the knife might be at my throat. Involuntarily I screamed. Heard the scream. Unrecognizable. An
animal's cry. I threw myself out into the corridor, bruising
my arm against the edge of the door. I heard the pounding of feet. But in the distance. Not behind me. I heard
David calling my name. And I ran, stumbling, toward the
sound of his voice.

We met at the bend of the corridor. He held the candle
away from my hair as he caught me against his side.

"It's Teles!" I gasped. "He's in her room!"

But he was not. Within minutes David had circled the
room, opened the closets, and come back to where I
stood, watching his candle throw light against the empty
mirror.

"Are you certain?" he asked grimly.

"I saw his face!" But I was already doubting myself. I
had been afraid, and in my fear I had imagined Teles.
Was that what had happened? David lowered the candle

toward the floor, and I heard him mutter something. Looking down, I saw a stain of yellow mud on the carpet. I
followed David as he moved slowly down the corridor in
the opposite direction from which he had come. I followed him closely enough to see the marks left by the
mud.

"He's gone down the side stairs," David said. "Probably
he's halfway back to the shed by now. I'm going after
him, Irene. You go back downstairs and tell the others
it's all right. When the inspector——"

"No." I said. My throat was so dry that I could scarcely
speak. "I won't let you go."

For a moment his face seemed to soften, and for that
moment he was the man I had known by moonlight. "I
have to go," he said in a low voice. "I've got to find out
what he was doing here. You know that, don't you?"

"Then let me go with you."

"That's impossible. I'm going to have to walk down
there. It's no use expecting to get the truck back there.
You can't——"

"I can."

"No." He paused. "Irene, you do know what you mean
to me, don't you? If there were some way I could get
you out of this house now and keep you out, I would.
Now go back to the others. Tell them. . . . Don't tell
them anything. Say that you screamed because you saw
your reflection in the mirror. Tell them I'm searching
Senhora's room, and after that I'm going to search the
house for her. MacGregor's an old man. They'll understand that I might think I couldn't take his word for her
not being here. That's all. Don't tell them anymore than
that. Whatever you do, don't mention having seen Teles."

"But you do believe I saw him."

"At first I thought you were imagining things, but the
mud convinced me."

"Do you think he knows where she is?"

David shrugged. "Listen, Irene. I've got to go down

there, and you must join the others. Keep them together if you can. I'm not sure about Kubler, but I think he'll help you. And, Irene. . . ."

"Yes?"

For a long moment we stood in silence, caught in the oval glow of the candlelight. And I knew that whatever he wanted to say, he could not say it.

"You'll need a flashlight," I said brusquely, stepping back into the shadows.

"I know my way," he said and put his hand on my arm. He did not look at me, nor did I look at him. Slowly his fingers slipped down to my wrist, and then, for a long moment, our hands met, palm to palm.

"Be careful," he said in a low voice. "For God's sake, be careful, Irene."

I repeated the words under my breath as he disappeared down the narrow flight of stairs. I remembered all too vividly the night I had run down those same stairs to meet him in the courtyard. The moonlight had made the night a silvered day. Now the candlelight was warm and golden. And what I felt for him had changed from silver to gold as well.

Holding the candle at arm's length, I went to the window overlooking the courtyard. But I could see nothing. I might have been staring into a void. Even the stone pig was not visible. The panes of glass rattled under the prodding of the wind, and the rain beat a wild tattoo. Pressing my hand against my mouth, I slowly turned and looked about me: at the drapes, spots of crimson in the flare of the candle flame; at the thin line of the hallway, narrowing itself into a black pencil-line of nothingness. I was no longer afraid. Even if Teles had not really left the house, even if he was hiding in one of the rooms, behind one of the closed doors, it did not matter. What mattered was the ache inside me, the burning of tears against my closing eyelids. Oh, God, why was it such a terrible thing to me that David should have gone without me?

Slowly I made my way back down the long corridor. Time seemed to have stopped inside my mind. It seemed that I had lived forever among these shadows. Fear and exhaustion had ceased to have any meaning to me. I knew that my hands and arms and clothing were caked with mud, that my face was blackened with soot. I had seen that in the mirror in Senhora's room in the moment before I had glimpsed Teles's face. Why he had been there did not interest me. I was numb. My body and my mind were numb—except for the ache inside my chest which had begun when David had disappeared down the stairs.

When I reached the top of the wide staircase, I began to hear their voices. Apparently they had stayed in the drawing room. There was something odd in that, surely. I had screamed. David had left them and not returned. Yet they had stayed where they were. Because he had told them to, or did they remain together out of fear? What did it matter? What did any of it matter?

I had no real reason to blow out my candle. Probably there was every reason not to. There were no lights burning in the hall. The candles that had been there had been taken into the drawing room. Yet I preferred the darkness. Perhaps in the darkness I could think. Slowly I groped my way down the marble stairs, one hand on the railing. By the time I reached the bottom step, I could hear their voices clearly, Claire's shrill and penetrating, William's gruff in response. Then Martin Kubler was saying; "No, we'll wait here—for another few minutes at least."

I caught a glimpse of them as I passed the door, moving soundlessly across the tiled floor in my soft-soled sandals. The candlelight cast a yellow glow on the frightened faces of the maids, who huddled together near the fireplace. Martin was standing in the center of the long room, his back to me. William and Claire were seated on the sofa, and I saw that he had his arm about her. The house-keeper was perched stiffly on the edge of a chair facing them. She was speaking, but I could not make out the words. I paused. David had told me to go to them, but he had been wrong. He had been wrong not to let me go with him.

The groping fingers of light illuminated the anteroom that led into the dining room. I saw the glitter of the crystal decanter and went to it. Slowly. Silently. The richness of the port was sweet in my mouth. I drained the glass and set the decanter back on its tray, my decision made. In a moment I was at the thick oak door that led outside. They were arguing now; William's voice was raised petulantly. I slid the latch down, and the door swung open. Rain battered me as I stepped outside. I could not see the truck until my hand touched the fender. If only the key had been left in the ignition. That was all that mattered now.

The cab smelled of grapes and gasoline. I felt for the key and found it there. The motor turned over with a rattling sound. I groped among the knobs protruding from the panel and found the light switch. The windshield wipers were inadequate to deal with the torrent of rain, but as the truck began to move, I did not think of that or the muddy roads ahead. I knew where David was going, and I had to get there. That was all that mattered.

I don't know whether the drive took minutes or hours. At the time it seemed like an indefinite nightmare. The first part went easily, although I could scarcely make out the twisting gravel road that led between the pines. But I reached the gate intact. There were only two choices then as far as roads were concerned. Straight ahead of me stretched the tarred road down which I had made my first approach to Alcombra. The other, the one I took, swerved to the left. The headlights caught the rich yellow of the mud. Once I was on it, I found it was like oil.

The truck skidded from one side of the narrow track to the other. I had no way of knowing what lay on either side, but I understood now why David had estimated that there was more chance of his reaching the shed through the vineyard on foot than in this way. Struggling to keep the wheel under control, I stepped as heavily as I could on the accelerator, determined not to bog down in the sea of mud even though the alternative might be to skid off the road completely.

Not until I saw the shed ahead of me did I realize that my teeth had been set so hard that my jaw ached, but only the warm flood of relief mattered. I switched off the motor without bothering to turn off the road. Lights glowed from the shed window. Whoever was there, I did not want to warn them. For a moment I simply leaned on the wheel, pressing my forehead against my arms, taking deep breaths to calm myself. It had been one thing to follow David here. It would be another to ruin whatever plan he had through my own carelessness. He did not even need to know I was here. If he was inside with Teles, I would not break in on them. I only had to know that he was all right. I simply had to be near him until this nightmare was over.

The wind buffeted me as I stepped down from the cab of the truck. I had switched off the lights, but the sound of the rain drumming on the tin roof of the shed told me I was even closer to it than I had guessed. The lights behind the dirty windows were too steady to come from candles. Ankle deep in mud, I made my way toward the lights. When one sandal was pulled from my foot, I kicked off the other and went on in my bare feet.

I stopped only when I had reached the corner of the long low building. Gasping to regain the breath the wind had whipped away, I wrenched back my long hair, wringing the water out of it to keep it from draining down over my face. I began to shiver uncontrollably as I moved to the first window, although whether from the bite of the wind on my wet skin or from a rising dread, I did not know.

The window was high. Only by taking hold of the sill and pulling myself up on the tips of my toes could I see inside. What I witnessed was a scene of horror. Directly across the room from me stood the mechanical press, illuminated by gas lamps that lined the walls. The press was round, the barrel composed of wooden staves with thin gaps between them. I knew that inside, the barrel was packed with trodden grape skins. When the press was not in use, there was a heavy wooden lid on the top. I had seen it there this afternoon. But now the lid was not visible, and I knew that it had been screwed down into the press by the turning of the long metal rods that projected from the rim of the barrel. As the rods were turned, the lip would be screwed tighter and tighter against the grape skins, squeezing the liquid out of them. Perhaps even before Teles stepped into view, I knew what was really happening.

He was naked to the waist, his dark skin glistening with sweat. As I watched with horrified fascination, he leaned against one of the metal rods and slowly began to turn it. Behind him his shadow moved grotesquely against the wall. Teles's face was toward me, and I could see the grim concentration in his dark eyes as he threw his entire strength against the rod. Over the sound of the wind and the pulsing beat of the rain on the tin roof, I heard the sharp click as the ratchet was engaged and the heavy lid was forced down farther against whatever lay beneath it.

I could only think that he must be stopped, and yet I am sure that I did not deliberately strike my hand against the window. At the time I thought that it was an accident, that I had lost my balance and that in my trying to regain it, my hand had hit the glass. But whatever the truth, I can still remember the shock of terror that I felt

as Teles, hearing the noise, looked up. Perhaps he could
not see me through the darkness beyond the room, but
his black eyes seemed to burn into mine. Slowly, with his
left hand, he reached across the top of the barrel and
without drawing his gaze from the window, twisted a
sort of latch. Only when he took his other hand off the
rod and started to move with a rough shambling gait
toward the door did I push myself away from the
window and start to run.

The mud was thick under foot, and I slid to the side
and nearly fell. By the time I had reached the corner
of the shed, I heard the door slam. Fear blinded me, or
perhaps it was the night. I could not see the truck.
Hesitating, I knew that I was lost. I felt the man's hands
on me, twisting my shoulders. I struggled, and it was
like a nightmare repeating itself. This was the man who
had been lurking in Senhora's room. The sour, acrid
odor of crushed grapes was the same. I felt the rough
texture of his shirt as he pulled me against him.

"Stop!" I cried. "Let me go!"

"Teles! What in hell do you think you're doing?"

It was David's voice. David's arm was about me. I sank
back against him, breathless. In the dim light sifting
through the dirty windows of the shed I saw Teles hunch
his shoulders and turn away from us. In a moment the
door of the shed slammed behind him.

"You little fool!" David muttered. "I told you not to
come."

"You've got to stop that man," I gasped, pulling myself
away from him. "He's working the press, and Senhora.
. . . I think he's killed her. I think her body is inside the
barrel. . . ."

I did not have to finish. Together we ran through the
mud to the shed. Teles had not bothered to bolt the door.
David tried to push me back, but I followed him inside.
The odor of fermenting grapes was overwhelming. Teles,
bent over the rod again, did not turn even when David

slammed the door behind us. The ratchet creaked into place, and the gas jets hissed.

"Teles!" David shouted.

The broad-backed man bent farther over the rod.

"Teles," David said again, this time in a low voice, "I want to talk to you."

"I can talk and work," the man muttered. "Why have you come back here at this time of the night? And the woman. It is no place for a woman to lurk about. How did I know that it was she? How did I know that it was not someone bent on doing damage to this property? It is my duty to protect——"

"Let me ask the questions, Teles," David said grimly. "Why are you working this press now?"

"The grapes must be processed," Teles replied, pulling the rod upward slowly with an effort that made his muscles strain. "It is not unusual for me to work at night during the vintage."

"I know that," David said sharply, "but not alone. Where are the men who should be helping you?"

Teles paused, the rod raised to the height of his shoulder. "They have refused," he said. "This press is dangerous, and I have told them so, since it is only fair that they should know. You saw the condition of the slats this afternoon. If one should burst. . . ." He shrugged. "It happened once five years ago. Perhaps you remember. Three men were killed, one of them decapitated. Not a pleasant sight, I can assure you."

"There are presses in the other sheds," David retorted. "I thought we had agreed that this one was not to be used."

"I do not mind the risk," Teles muttered, pushing the metal rod downward.

"Teles!" Leaving me, David went toward the press. "An hour ago you were at Alcombra. You were seen in Senhora's room. I want you to tell me why you were there."

"Stand back," Teles warned. With an effort he pushed the iron rod into its lowest position, and the ratchet clicked again as the lid descended lower into the cask. "I have told you that this press is not safe."

"If it explodes, it won't make much difference where I am standing," David said grimly. "I think if you were really concerned with our safety, you would stop working that thing."

"Perhaps," the man said, "it would be simpler if you and the lady would leave."

"Wouldn't you rather explain why you were in Senhora's room to us than to the police?" David said in a low voice.

The estate manager stared at him blankly. "You are threatening me, Mr. Ashor?"

"Senhora is missing," David said. "Do you know where she is?"

"Why should I know where she is, Mr. Ashor?" There was something taunting about the man's voice. He began to lift the metal rod upward.

"Because," David said in a loud voice, "she is your wife and has been for the last ten years."

Teles must have loosened his hold on the rod, for suddenly it began to spin. He threw himself on it, holding it in position with all his strength. Sweat poured down his swarthy face, and on his right hand I saw a red gash where the rod had struck it. Teles began to laugh wildly. The sound made me grow cold inside.

"You are dreaming, Mr. Ashor," he said, taking great gulps of air between each word.

"No," David responded quietly. "It is true. Lady Stewart told me about it two years ago. I know that it was intended to be secret, but she found you once in Senhora's room, and the truth came out. She was angry. You knew her feelings on the subject of Senhora. Senhora's only allegiance was supposed to be to my great-aunt. She told you that she would dismiss both of you if you attempted to live together as man and wife."

For a moment there was silence except for the hissing of the lights and the pounding of the rain against the tin roof. Teles remained motionless, holding the rod in a down position. "She was an evil woman," he muttered finally. "She wanted to control the lives of everyone about her. And in return for what? A few *escudos*."

"Is that why you stole from the collection?" David asked. "To get from her what you thought you deserved?"

I stared at him, puzzled. How could he have known that anything was missing? I had not told him. For some absurd reason that I could not remember, I had not told him.

"My great-aunt told me she suspected that was what was happening," David said as though in answer to my unspoken question. "She told me that the day before she died. She intended to make a list——"

"She made one," I said.

David turned toward me, grim-faced. "You should have told me," he said. "A good many things would have made sense before this if you had told me." His voice hardened. "Was that why she talked to you that night?"

"Yes."

"And did you check the list?"

"The next morning. Five pieces were missing. I—I have one of them here." I dug in my pocket for the ring and held it out to him. He backed toward me, not taking his eyes off Teles, and took it from me.

"Where did you find it?" he asked.

"Senhora claimed to have found it in Claire Stewart's bedroom," I said.

"Have you seen this ring before, Teles?" David asked, stretching out his hand.

"I do not have to answer your questions."

"If you do not give me answers, you will give them to the police. I think I understand now, Teles. You began to steal from the collection when you knew my great-

aunt was going to die. You must have felt very safe—
until she decided to have an inventory made."

"Senhora didn't want me to come," I said, following
David closer to the cask. "I heard her tell Lady Stewart
that she could make the inventory herself. She wanted
me to be sent away."

The flash of hatred in Teles's eyes as they met mine
stunned me. I looked past him at the cask, its wooden
staves straining against the rusting iron bands that held
them in place.

"Senhora failed you, didn't she?" David asked. "You
counted on her to have more influence on a dying woman
than she did have. Miss Haverlock stayed."

Suddenly I remembered the piece of granite tumbling
down past me as I stood in the vineyard the afternoon of
Marian's death. Had that been Teles's attempt to put an
end to the threat of discovery which my presence at
Alcombra presented? And Marian's death. Was that. . . ?

David voiced the words as though our minds were
working in unison. "You killed my mother," he said.
"You thought that only Miss Haverlock was in the wing
that afternoon. It was dark because of the storm. You
saw a woman, and you killed her."

Teles made a strangling noise deep in his throat, and I
saw his hands grip the metal rod as though he wanted
to rip it out of the cask.

"Someone took the list out of my room the night your
mother was killed," I said in a low voice to David,
touching his arm. "Senhora returned it."

"She wouldn't go along with you, would she?" David
said to Teles. "I've known Senhora for a good many
years. She's capable of a good deal, but not of murder.
She fought against what you were doing to cover the
thefts, didn't she? And in the end she was more of a
liability than an asset. She couldn't even manage to put
the blame on Claire. That was why you tried to burn the
wing down tonight, wasn't it? You must have left here

as soon as I had gone. And when that failed, Senhora had to die, didn't she? She was the only person who could give evidence against you. What have you done with your wife's body, Teles? Is it in the press?"

Pushing all his weight against the metal rod, Teles suddenly groped out with one hand and grabbed a hammer from the floor. I saw him strike at one of the bulging staves. And strike again. In the same moment the door behind me was thrown open to the roar of the storm and someone fell against me, knocking me to the floor. Over the sound of the storm came the thunder of an explosion, and the scream of a man.

It was Jerez lying on top of me. I saw his face as I crawled free into a sea of cold slippery grape skins and a thick liquid that was like blood. Coated with wine, I pushed myself upright. The blast of the exploding cask had thrown David against the wall, but the flying staves had not struck him, as they had Teles. We stared in horror at the body of the man on the floor, his neck nearly severed from his body. Beside him, half-buried in the remains of the pressed grapes, was the mutilated body of Senhora.

It was dawn when we walked back to Alcombra. Above the hedges and the pines the house loomed over us, drenched in the faint white light of early morning. We came up through the vineyards, pausing sometimes, but never to look behind us. It was as though we both understood that if we did not look back, the deepening light would drive away the shadows in our minds. When we had started up the terraced slopes, I had been numb inside and so physically exhausted that it had been an effort to move. Jerez had gone back to the house with the inspector in his car, knowing perhaps that David and I needed to heal one another, and that to do that we had to be alone.

As we reached the dew-drenched lawns of the house,

I felt life spring up inside me, as warm as the tentative touch of the sun's rays on my back. David's arm was about my waist, and my head was on his shoulder. We moved so slowly, as though we were one person, that the peacocks did not seem to notice us. Only one, his white breast flaring, spread his tail feathers as we passed, flaunting the mosaic of his colors.

There was so much that we could have said. Yet there was no need for either of us to speak a word. It was, I knew, a fresh beginning. The past could never be forgotten, but it had already begun to fade. Philip? The woman who had loved him had been another woman, unsure of herself, uncertain of what she wanted from life. I felt as though I had been reborn. The future held the fulfillment I had only dreamed of before. David. I raised my head, and our eyes met. The scent of flowers hung heavy in the morning air as we turned into one another's arms. Somewhere the call of a peacock broke the silence, and for the first time the sound came to me not as a scream but as a cry of joy.